# a little shop of horrors

# Rod Fleming

Published in 2016 by PlashMill Press, Scotland.



ISBN: 978-0-9565007-8-6 (print)

ISBN: 978-0-9572612-8-0 (epub)

*All illustrations by Rod Fleming*

*http://rodfleming.com*

*https://.amazon.com/author/rodfleming*

For my dear friend Andreia Guerrero; a muse, a wayward spirit, my confidant and my collaborator. My world would be much less rich without you.

# Contents

# The Tarot Cards

Rachel Sutherland was thirty-eight years old, and had already brought three children into the world. She pondered this as she looked at her naked body, reflected in the mirror on the wardrobe in her bedroom. Not bad, she thought, not bad at all. She piled up the extravagant mane of thick dark blonde hair that she always wore long, and turned her body from side to side, examining every contour with practised eye.

She was not what anyone would have called skinny; she was rather short, and her body was full and curvaceous, but still firm and shapely. She smiled. She knew plenty of other mothers of her age who had ost their figures completely. She purred like a cat and looked into the deep brown eyes reflected in the mirror. She leaned closer to the glass. Perhaps a few more lines there, perhaps the freckles that dusted her nose were more prominent, but still…

Satisfied, she dropped her hair, shook her head and began to dress. One must not be smug, she scolded herself mentally. Remember what her grandmother had always said: 'Pride cometh before a fall.' But why should she dread those words? Why should she not be content with what she had – a husband who loved her and never failed to provide, three beautiful children, and the body of a woman ten years younger? It would do for now, she thought, it would do for now.

She finished dressing and left her bedroom. The corridor outside was panelled in pine matchboard, and the rooms each had a number These came from the First World War, when the house had been used as a convalescent home for young officers who had been wounded in the trenches.

It was a warm house, and a content one. It had passed down through the generations of Sutherlands, even though the family had decamped to London nearly fifty years ago. They had always kept it on, their little retreat buried in the heart of Angus, as a holiday home, a place where they could meet up and be together in peace.

The Sutherlands were close, but in recent years, they had rarely come to this house. Now here they were again, Rachel, and her two sisters Jenny and Felicity.

There were two years between each of the sisters; Rachel was the eldest, then Jenny, then Felicity. Of course they never called Felicity by that name to her face; she would have huffed like a cat. Since childhood, Rachel's youngest sister had shunned her given name, and lacking any diminutive that was both feminine and to her taste, had settled on Felix, and so she had been ever since.

Felix and Rachel were strikingly similar and had often been taken for twins; Felix had the same curvy body, the same golden skin, the same shock of hair. Even when you were close up the resemblance was striking; they had the same high cheekbones, the same fine nose, the same even white teeth. But there was no mistaking the eyes; whereas Rachel's were a deep chestnut brown full of red and gold, Felix' eyes were pale blue and shone as if they were lit from behind.

Rachel had always had a twinge of jealousy about her little sister; when they were teenagers, Felix had often purloined Rachel's clothes, which fitted her like a glove. But somehow, to Rachel's eyes, Felix managed to make them look – not better, but sexier. It piqued Rachel, that did, and she was glad to see that now, as her mirror had just confirmed, her body was still as fresh as her sister's.

Jenny, on the other hand, was tall and saturnine, and didn't look like her sisters at all. She was slender and elegant; cool, and a little detached. She was married and had two children, but unlike Rachel had decided to return to work and was studying a refresher course.

Felix had never married. She had had a burning desire to prove herself and had thrown herself at her professional career, with, to her great credit, much success.

It was because of Felix that they were all there, together; Felix had Trouble. The kind of trouble that was spoken of only in hushed tones and in quiet corners and never in front of Felix herself. A trouble which had obliged Felix to spend many months in psychiatric care, and an instruction to take things easy for a long while.

In point of fact, Felix, after working flat out all her adult life, having dedicated herself to her career, had had a mental collapse when the man with whom she had been living for several years had simply walked out of her life one day. He said that he wanted a family, children, a 'real home' and that he was fed up with a life snatched between late nights and early starts and working weekends.

He left Felix for a much younger woman, hardly more than a teenager. She had been his office secretary and Felix, who had always appeared to the world to have enormous confidence in her attractiveness, not to say her sexual powers, and in her ability to control her destiny, had been totally demolished.

She fell into deep depression. It was as if her whole life had been a stack of cards that had suddenly fallen apart. Nothing – not work, not family, and none of the pleasures of life seemed to mean anything at all to her after her collapse.

In the end, Felix made several attempts on her own life. She had always been a poor swimmer and had almost succeeded in killing herself when she had thrown herself into the sea near Hastings; only by the fact that her attempt was witnessed and rescue close at hand had catastrophe been avoided.

After months of therapy, however, Felix was pronounced, if not cured, then at least on the mend. Her doctors had suggested to the family that it might be a good idea to take her to a place where she only had good memories, so that she could rebuild the inner strength that she seemed to have lost entirely. However, they cautioned that it was possible that she might relapse, and the family must ensure that she was never left alone long enough to make another attempt at suicide.

Rachel and Jenny sat down together and decided that the best thing to do for their little sister was for all three of them, with their families and cats and dogs, to decamp to the old place in Angus for the summer, just to relax and to…well, just to be. There they could keep an eye on her, and hopefully complete her cure.

Felix had at first baulked at the idea, but after some protest she agreed. She was pretty used to her big sisters trying to sort out her life for her, and six months before she would have firmly told them no, she would rather spend a holiday in Venice or trekking in the Himalayas. But she was exhausted after her illness and had not the strength to resist the concerted onslaught of two determined sisters. So now here they all were, in the little house in a snug glen not far from Brechin in Angus.

Rachel stepped out of the door of the house and her hair lit up in a blaze under the sun. The balmy morning air was all around her, a gentle breeze stirred the tall beeches that sheltered the house, and collared doves cooed in their branches. Jenny was already out, lounging on a sunbed, her skin even now the dark brown of summer. Rachel could never tan like that; her skin was fair and golden, like Felix, but Jenny could soak up the sun till she became the colour of polished mahogany, with no ill effect, it seemed.

'I'm going shopping,' said Rachel. 'Want to come?'

Her sister sniffed and raised her head a little. 'Nope, gotta get my ration,' she said, waving an elegant hand in the direction of the sun. Then, with a wicked twinkle in her eye as she regarded Rachel over the tops of her sunglasses, she added, 'Bring back some ice-cream, though.'

Jenny was perfectly aware that items such as *ice-cream* had long since been excised from her sister's diet.

'Felix about?' asked Rachel, after sticking her tongue out at Jenny.

Jenny shook her head and let it fall back on the pillow. 'Not up yet.'

'Keep an eye on the kids, then,' said Rachel, and went to her car.

'Don't be late,' called her sister after her. 'The boys will be here by one.'

Rachel climbed into her car and drove off towards Brechin.

Junk shops were a great weakness with Rachel; she could not pass one by, and though she never spent a lot of money, she always bought something. So her house had become full of trinkets and strange flotsam from all over the world that had washed up in some gloomy and dusty cavern.

That morning, while walking up the steep High Street in Brechin, her delighted eye fell upon a hand-painted sign she had not seen before. 'Antiques and Curios,' it said, and underneath was an arrow pointing along a narrow vennel.

Without hesitating Rachel plunged into the coolth of the vaulted passage and, following it, came out into a little paved lane between two high walls. A few yards more and there was an open door to her left; she stuck her head into the dim interior and there espied an Aladdin's Cave, a dusty hoard of the bizarre, the unusual, the useless, the old and the forgotten.

An hour later, already late for lunch, she came out again, her eyes gleaming and her bag fat with the treasure she had struck.

By the time she got back to the house, she found Jenny's prediction had been correct – the boys, Martin and John, Jenny and Rachel's respective husbands, had indeed arrived. They had driven up together and, having stopped overnight in the Lake District, had arrived in good time for lunch – and both of them roundly berated Rachel for making them wait for it. But she rose above their ribbing with her usual ease, flirted with Martin, and then cuddled her husband. She even forgot about the junk-shop in Brechin in her excitement.

Lunch was a lively affair, as tended to be the case with the Sutherlands; five adults and five children, together with several dogs, eating lunch at a makeshift trestle table on the lawn.

It was a fine family party and it broke up slowly, everyone feeling content, at about four o'clock. Rachel and Jenny were left sitting together at the table. From the distance came sounds of children and the occasional adult voice advising caution, or encouraging high jinks.

'So, what took you, sis,' asked Jenny at length, her long eyes narrow. 'Fancy man in Brechin?'

'That will be right!' exclaimed Rachel. 'I found a new junk shop.'

'You and your junk shops! What rubbish have you dug up this time?' Junk shops were not in Jenny's line, but she was reluctantly interested in Rachel's discoveries. Just occasionally she turned up something that Jenny would have given her eye teeth for, but then

Jenny could never have tolerated all that dust and mustiness.

'Ah-ha! You'll never guess!'

'Well then *show* me,' hissed Jenny impatiently.

Rachel fetched her bag and fished out the packet which was still bulging there.

'What is it – a book?'

'No – better. Look.'

Rachel unwrapped the package and handed it to Jenny. It was a brown leather-bound box, about seven inches by five. 'Open it,' she said.

Jenny took the box from Rachel, her face an expression of mild distaste. 'What queer leather binding,' she said. 'It has a strange texture. What's inside, I wonder.' Jenny lifted the top from the box and tipped the contents into her hand. She laughed. 'What on earth have you got here?'

'Tarot cards,' explained Rachel, her eyes flashing with excitement.

'Tarot cards? You're not into that sort of thing, are you?' laughed Jenny. 'Somehow I've never seen you as a dark and mysterious fortune teller. More my line, I should have thought.' And she made an arch face, fanning out the cards before her.

Rachel laughed too. Most people thought Jenny was cool and aloof, but actually she was the joker of the family, always teasing.

'I don't know, though,' Jenny went on. 'I can't see me doing it either. All that incense – it must make so much *dust!*'

'Yes, but you're obsessive,' laughed Rachel. 'Look, the cards are hand painted. They must be very old. And the work is – well, it's really beautiful. At least I think it is.'

'Weird, more like,' replied Jenny. 'Whoever drew these had a screw or two loose. But you're right, they *are* old and they must be quite unusual. Probably worth a bob or two.'

'Unusual? Unique, I'd have thought. I wonder who they belonged to – who painted them.'

Jenny looked intently at her sister. 'Well, shall we?' she asked.

'Shall we what?'

Jenny leaned forward. 'Read the cards of course, silly. Don't you want to know if there's a tall dark stranger in your future?'

'Oh, but I don't know how – '

Just at that, Jenny's eldest daughter, Alison, who was eleven, came up. 'What are those,' she gasped, her eyes wide. 'Tarot cards?'

'Oh, you know about such things, do you,' asked her mother suspiciously. 'You watch too much television, my dear.'

'No, a girl at school has a set. May I see? Oh, they're nothing like these. These ones are really beautiful. Do you know how to read them, Auntie Rachel?'

'No I don't,' replied her aunt, who was still not sure about being called *Auntie.* 'You're not telling me that you *do,* are you?'

'Yes. Well anyway my friend showed me. It's fun, you'll see. I'll show you,' said the little girl and pouted at her mother, who threw up her hands in mock despair.

Rachel caught her breath. She had not hesitated to buy the cards, but the thought of doing a reading – of seeing what they might have to tell – disturbed her for reasons that she could not place. It suddenly struck her that in some queer way the cards had brought the night out into the sunny afternoon.

'Isn't it – isn't that sacrilegious or something?' she said.

Jenny scoffed. 'Rachel! You haven't seen the inside of a church since the day you were married. Your house is full of old bits of pews and junk from churches. Since when did such things bother you?'

But Rachel was eyeing the cards, which lay in a stack on the table between her and her sister with an expression of severe distaste. It seemed to her that the air had become chill and that the sun had been veiled; there was something – no, she could not name it – something that, well, *horrified* her about the cards and all at once she found herself wishing, more fervently than she could ever remember, that for once she had resisted the impulse to buy.

Her voice failed her for a few moments. 'I'm not sure I want to know – that I want to know the future,' she said at last, quietly.

'Oh, Rachel, you don't actually believe in all that nonsense, do you? Next thing there'll be fairies at the bottom of the garden. Have another glass of wine and snap out of it. Alison is just dying to show us, aren't you, sweetie?'

It had occurred to Rachel – despite her nature, as she was not inclined to ponder the profundities of life – that it was possible that something altogether nastier than fairies might be lurking in the shadows at the bottom of the garden, and she shivered at the thought.

Then she shrugged, although a cold, gnawing sensation persisted deep within her, and she smiled at her niece. How mean of her it would be to spoil a little girl's fun. And Alison was such a delightful child, the image of her mother. So she shook herself and firmly put her silly reservations behind her.

'Yes, all right. Go on, then,' she said.

'We really don't have to, Auntie, if you don't want,' said Alison, her voice concerned. Rachel reached out and drew the little girl to her, cuddling her and drawing strength from her slender young body.

'No, darling, you go ahead. You show me how it's done.'

'Well, you start like this. You shuffle the cards.'

'Why me? Why not you?'

'Because I'm going to do you first, so you have to shuffle the cards, silly. It's better like that. And anyway, my hands are too small. I'll drop them.'

In the space of those few moments, the frost had returned to Rachel's heart at the thought of touching the cards, which now seemed to be emanating an aura of pure malevolence. She was not the sort of person who is easily turned from her course and she was getting angry with herself.

'*Do come on,*' she thought, in the same tone she'd use talking to a recalcitrant horse. 'You're being silly. They're just cards with pictures on. It's only a game.' So, shaking herself again, Rachel extended her hand to pick up the cards, even though her every impulse was to turn and run from that place, to burn those cards, tear them up, throw them in the river, whatever, but not to ask them, not to see…

'Oh, Rachel, what on earth has got into you today?' exclaimed Jenny, breaking Rachel's train of thought, for which the latter was grateful. 'I'm beginning to think you're coming down with something. Give me the cards and I'll go first.'

So saying she reached out and took the pack of cards and began to shuffle them, her impossibly elegant and beautiful hands making those exquisite motions that were so captivating.

'Doesn't she *see?*' asked Rachel of herself. 'Is it really just me?' Somehow, to her eyes the cards seemed to be giving out a shadow, darkening the world around them, even as a lantern gives out a light that illuminates the darkness.

Rachel watched the cards with mounting horror; but she could no more take her eyes from them than she could do the thing that she wanted to do more than any other; to run and run and run, away from that creeping darkness and horror that now seemed to surround those beautiful hands shuffling the cards.

She listened apprehensively as Alison explained how to cut the cards, and how to lay them out on the table. 'You put *that* one here,' she pointed, 'And you say, "This is the King who governs all things." You leave them face down, Mummy, you mustn't look yet. Now, you take the next and put it to the right and say, "This is the Queen" and then put one on the left and say, 'This is the Minister". Then you take the next two and put them above the King and say, "This is Fire and this is Air," and then you put two underneath and say, "This is Earth and this is Water." See?'

At length Jenny had finished and the cards were laid out, face down, on the table in front of her. 'And now I turn them over?' she asked.

'Yes. In the order you laid them out,' nodded Alison.

A hush that was almost palpable seemed to flow all around them and it was all Rachel could do to stop herself from shaking as she watched her sister flip over the first card. She gasped aloud when she saw it was the XIII of Trumps, Death.

'*Oh, my God!*' she cried.

'Don't worry, Auntie,' exclaimed Alison. 'It doesn't really mean death, it just means that there is going to be a change. It's a very powerful card, especially as the King.'

'Rachel, love,' came Jenny's voice from across the table. 'Are you all right?'

'Yes, I'm fine,' said Rachel, but inside her the pounding horror thumped at her temples. She could hardly bear to watch as her sister turned over the rest of the cards, but no power in the world could have made her drag her eyes away.

'So, what do they say?' demanded Jenny when she had finished.

'Well,' said Alison, 'I'm not very good at this part, but there's going to be a change in your life. See, that's what this card means. And there's going to be something else – something to do with water, I think – '

'A cruise with a tall dark stranger?' came a man's voice, unexpected, from behind. Rachel started and, looking up, saw Martin slip up behind his daughter and grab her around the waist.

'What a proper coven of witches we have here!' he exclaimed as Alison wriggled in delight. 'So *this* is what you get up to when there's no men about.'

Jenny pulled out the chair next to her and her husband sat down, his daughter on his knee. Rachel smiled at him. Suddenly the oppressive menace that she had been feeling had been blown away like a puff of smoke by the arrival of this big, bluff, good-natured man who reminded her of a Labrador retriever, totally devoted and loyal to Jenny.

'Well, shall we do a reading for you, since you've caught us in the act?' asked Jenny.

'No, thanks,' came Martin's reply. 'I don't like any of that stuff. It's as likely to trip you up with trickery and fraud as to tell you something true. I'll have nothing to do with it. But you go on, if you like.'

'No, that's all right,' said Jenny. 'I think we'd had enough anyway. But my, you *are* a dark one – fourteen years married and I never knew you felt that way.'

'It's me fey Cornish granny coming out in me,' laughed Martin. 'No, it's nothing, really, it just makes my skin creep a bit.'

Rachel stretched and looked at her watch; whatever the spell that had been laid by the cards was, it had vanished, and in her trademark fashion, she would get on with life now. The table had to be cleared and there was dinner to be thought of. As she did so, her youngest son, Peter, came running up.

'Look Mummy, I found a frog,' he cried. Suddenly all attention was turned to him and the Tarot cards lay forgotten on the table.

Rachel rose and began to clear away the last of the lunchtime debris.

'Where is everyone else?' she asked, looking around and noticing, for the first time, that several of the company were missing.

'Felix and John have taken the dogs for a walk. Down by the old quarry, they said. Here, let me help with that,' said Martin. He caught the look in Rachel's eye and went on, his voice reassuring. 'Oh, don't worry, Rachel, John will make sure she doesn't – I mean, he'll take care of her.'

Rachel nodded and smiled, swallowing this new fear that had mounted within her. She continued to clear away, leaving the Tarot cards as they had been.

It was over an hour later when Rachel came back out of the house; the sun had moved behind the trees and the heat had gone out of the day. In the middle distance, a rumble of thunder presaged a violent break in the weather. She had completely forgotten about the Tarot reading, and the feeling of deep unquiet which had filled her.

Now she realised, clucking herself, that she had left the cards out. She looked up, saw above her the gathering ramparts of cloud and went to the table where the cards were still lying as they had been left.

She was about to sweep them up when something stayed her hand and she looked again at the cards. Instantly all the terror and horror that she had felt before flooded back into her soul and all power to resist was drained from her. Around her the table, the chairs, the lawn and the house, everything, seemed to be consumed by a gathering, impenetrable mirk. Looking at the cards a thought took shape in her mind, a thought that she struggled to suppress but could not, a thought that chilled her deep to her core.

'This is not Jenny's reading, it's mine,' her mind screamed. It couldn't be, how could it? Jenny had shuffled the cards. But of course – it all made sense – the shop she had never noticed before, the way she had found the cards moments after she had entered its musty gloom, the way that she had put them down at first only to return and return again before finally buying; the way that she had been filled with the weird horror she had felt earlier – no, those cards might have been shuffled by Jenny, but they were speaking to *her*. They had sought her out, they had something to say – to her.

But what did they mean? She knew nothing of Tarot, and Alison knew only what a schoolgirl does; to her it was a parlour game. What *were* these cards – what were they trying to tell her?

She looked at them, her heart pounding. Here was Lust, showing a woman, naked, riding a mythic lion, her body writhing on the powerful beast, her hand holding a leash about its neck. Rachel was shocked by the image, but she shook herself and looked at the next, Sorrow, which showed terrible blades hacking at a beautiful rose blossom whose petals dropped one by one. But surely they were just pictures; and in any case she could not make sense of them.

She realised that her hands were shaking; she scolded herself for being so silly and forced herself to look at the cards again. Certainly they were fine work, she thought, dissembling to herself as much as she knew how, wondering pointlessly about the unknown artist who had created them, and for whom?

Why, she could see pictures within the pictures, they had depth, they seemed – they seemed so real.

And then, with a feeling of remounting horror that rose chokingly through her body, Rachel realised that in spite of her effort to resist them, before her eyes the images on the cards were changing. They were showing her something.

'Great God,' her mind told her, though she tried hard not to listen, 'They know I can't read them so they're going to show me!' She struggled to avert her eyes but she could not. She was rooted to the spot, rigid with terror, like a rabbit before a cat.

Rachel slid helplessly down onto a chair. One of her cards had turned into a whirling vortex of deep blue that seemed to drag her in and another, Change, was glowing brightly. It showed a coiled serpent; from its upper loop came an intense light that almost hurt her eyes. Her other cards were changing too. Her Past, the lovers, had transformed from a wedding scene, to a vision of a couple on a bed. She saw a woman, her arms and legs wrapped tightly around the body of a man, her head thrashing from side to side in the moment of her ecstasy, her thick blonde hair like a carpet. But who she was Rachel could not be sure, nor who was the man.

Lust had changed too, subtly – she could see that the woman on the lion's back was no longer a stylised image, but a real one. She thought at first it was herself; and then she realised that it was not she, but Felix, depicted there, her long hair flowing down the animal's back, her crystal blue eyes gazing out at Rachel, thick with envy and lust.

Then Rachel looked again at Sorrow, and instead of seeing an image of swords hacking at a rose, she found herself looking into a serene blue-green. Slowly the image expanded until it consumed the cards, the table, the lawn and all other; the greeny blue was everywhere and Rachel began to shiver with a terrible cold that froze her to her bones.

About her in the blue, shapes began to solidify, great streamers of green rising up towards a bright light high above. And then, most awful of all, Rachel perceived a figure, the body of a woman silhouetted against the sparkling surface of the water high above. She was naked, her skin pale blue, her arms outstretched like a crucifix, her legs entwined by grasping green tendrils of weed, her shock of golden hair like a halo around her head, her eyes closed in death.

Rachel looked closely, her heart pounding, cold sweat starting on her brow, the knot in the pit of her stomach twisting bitterly within her. Who was that woman – *who was she?* She must know, she must.

And then somehow, as if to answer her, a cool and green light illuminated the face, the eye-closed face, that seemed to be smiling in eternal serenity –

*'My God, it's Felix!'*

Rachel screamed and at the same time a gust of wind flicked over the cards on the table. The dreadful vision instantly disappeared, leaving her alone.

'Felix! *Felix!*' she cried.

Jenny, who heard her scream, came running out of the house.

'Oh Jenny – I just saw – the cards – they showed me – Oh, but where is Felix?'

'Why, she's gone to the old quarry with John and the dogs,' Jenny blurted out, completely nonplussed. 'But...'

'I have to go,' gasped Rachel. 'I have to go – Felix is a terrible swimmer, and John simply can't!'

Rachel, her hair streaming out behind her, ran off up the path towards the quarry. As she ran she yelled out her sister's name again and again. Behind her, the forgotten Tarot cards were strewn about the table and on the grass. As the first drops of rain fell on them with fat lazy plashes, the inks and watercolour of the designs flowed together until they were spoiled.

After an age of pounding along a path that seemed to extend itself as she ran along it, breathless gasps racking her, Rachel reached the old quarry. At first she could see no-one. And then John came towards her with a queer look on his face, his head hanging.

'What's happened!' demanded Rachel, distraught. 'Where is Felix?'

'Nothing's happened,' said John, and glanced back over the water.

'You're *lying!* John, why are you lying? What have you done – where is she? Felix! Oh my God, *Felix!*'

With that final cry, Rachel dropped her light summer frock and kicked off her sandals. Evading her husband's attempt to catch her she leapt into the cool clear water of the pool. There was the weed, but where was Felix? There, look, what was that?

She must go down, deeper...But the water was so cold...she had not thought it would be so *cold*...The deep blue was all around her and even her skin appeared blue...She felt the clammy tendrils of the weed catch at her limbs and then a terrible sob convulsed her body...

Jenny, who had been following at a more leaisurely place, half-amused by her sister's antics, arrived a few minutes later to find John at the edge of the water, shouting and gesticulating. Felix was approaching from the nearby wood, where the dogs were tied to a stump.

By far the strongest swimmer in the family, Jenny quickly dived in. She found her sister's naked body, twelve feet down, twining weed about her ankles, her arms outstretched and a look of total serenity on her face; but it was too late. She dragged – not without risk to herself – Rachel's lifeless husk to the surface and they tried, all of them, to revive her, but without success.

By the time the ambulance arrived, it was obvious that she was dead.

Jenny moved her family into a hotel, unable to stay at the house. After the funeral, she found Felix and John together.

'John has been such a friend these last few days,' said Felix, quietly.

Jenny glanced at John but he turned his eyes away. She looked hard at her sister and saw in her blue, blue eyes betrayal and with it, terrible remorse. In a flash she realised what John and Felix had been doing that afternoon; she knew now the reason for the queer look on John's face. She knew why Felix had suddenly appeared from behind those bushes, all innocence and she knew why the dogs had been tied to the stump of a tree.

The realisation of the enormity of her sister's offence swept over her. 'You – you – both of you – you were...you were...My God, how *could* you!' she whispered, aghast.

Felix turned her luminescent eyes on her sister. 'Oh Jenny, don't be such a prude, please. Don't bring that up now. Do you think I haven't cried *my* floods of tears? I loved Rachel too. You know I almost thought it was funny when she came running up and jumped into that dreadful pool – and then I realised...How was I to know...What could I do...You know I can hardly even keep myself afloat...As if I'd ever swim there!'

*'You little bitch!'* snapped Jenny, cutting her short. She slapped Felix, hard, on the cheek.

She drew back, shaking, her face pale with rage. 'May you rot in hell! *Both of you!*' she hissed, shaking her head, still not able to believe what she had just found out. And then she turned her back on them, the tears streaming down her face.

A month later, by the mutual agreement of the joint owners, Quarry House, near to Brechin in Angus, was put up for sale.

*I dramatised this story from tragic events that took place at a quarry in Angus called the Border Hole. A group of teenagers had gone swimming in it.*

*In quarries, which can be deep, the water is usually completely still. In summer the water near the surface may become pleasantly warm enough for swimming, but a metre or so below it remains close to freezing.*

*Several of the swimming party got into difficulties when they became suddenly chilled; one succumbed and drowned. His body was recovered by divers.*

*The quarry was later filled in.*

# The Ashes

The air had become cool, now, thought Ian Gillespie, scratching his stubbled cheek as he swung open the door of the car. Crisp and filled with the scent of earth and pine resin. In the slowly gathering light the formless black band of the trees had already begun to assume texture and colour. Above them the looming whaleback of Ben Aldui rose grey and foreboding, and behind its rolling brow he knew that the early day shone blue and clear. It might be chill now, but it would be hot enough all right by noon, thought Ian.

He got out of the car and stretched. It had been a long drive, begun in the dark hours of a late summer pre-dawn. He had left the softly curved form of his wife plunged deep into sleep, savouring the scent of her before he silently slipped from the bedroom they had shared for so long.

He was instantly aroused by the memory and he could almost smell her now...then he shook himself.

'Half awake, only,' he muttered. 'Some coffee'll soon mend that.' He went to the boot of the car and opened it, reaching in for the flask of coffee that he had carefully packed in there an hour and a half before.

The coffee tasted good and he felt the warmth rush through him. As he sipped it, he heard the swish of tyres on the gravel road that led up from the end of the tarmac, six miles further down the glen. He turned. It was Scott, as he had expected.

Scot was tall and thin with a balding brown head and monkeyish features. He stepped lightly from his car, a Land Rover, and strode purposefully to where Ian was standing.

Pleasantries quickly completed, the pair of them sipped their coffee as they looked around in the gathering light. It was always this way; it had been for years. Once they'd have had a cigarette with their coffee, never passing a word until the ritual was complete. But now they just drank their coffee in silent communion.

'Brought everything?' asked Scott at last. It was not a question – he knew perfectly well that Ian was the type who would have forgotten nothing. It was merely a way to break the silence, the slight strangeness that separated two men who knew each other so well.

'Aye,' Ian replied and glanced back towards his car. 'It's all in there.'

Scott nodded and then looked up. 'It's going to be a roaster,' he said. 'Best get going before the sun gets too high, or we'll be cooked alive.'

They threw the last slops of coffee down and repacked the flask. Then Ian swung his rucksack from the boot of the car and slipped it over his shoulders. He followed Scott, as he made toward the corner of the little car park with the stone collection box that had long since been broken open and left so, and the start of the path that led up, through the woods, onto the hill.

The day had gathered rapidly and the light, even in the shade of the forest, was strong enough to see the bleached-bone white roots that snaked across the jet black earth, slippery-moist and treacherous. As the slope steepened and the men settled into their stride, their breathing deepened, great draughts filled with the heady pine scent, the mouldy smell from the soil disturbed under their boots, the freshness of snapped blades of grass. This morning two men strode up the pine-scented path, but it had not always been so; once there had been three, and they had thought themselves inseparable.

They had met at University in Edinburgh, purely by chance, more years before than they liked to admit. Their first meeting was at a drunken party, after which Scott and Ian had rescued the third, a lanky bespectacled American named Tom, from drowning – or arrest.

He had he slipped and fallen into the fountain in Princes Street Gardens at three in the morning while trying to perform *Singing in the Rain* – and no business he'd had being there either, as the park gates are locked at sunset. They'd had to be quick on their toes too, for a passing police car had seen the incident and its occupants had given chase.

Whether it was youth, or exuberance, or the fact that the police were not really interested in three students up to harmless high-jinks, no-one knew, but still they had escaped a cold night in Fettes Row's cells. Ian could still remember the squelch, squelch that Tom's soaked shoes made on the pavement as they ran.

It was not long before the pair of walkers reached the edge of the forest, where it gave onto open moorland, and then they struck up direct, up the steep slope towards the crest of the ridge nearly six hundred feet above. The path was still clearly marked through the heather by the boots of countless others who had walked this way. They pulled up, heads down, sweat beginning to break, breath rasping on their lungs. At the top they stopped, and let their bodies catch up.

On the other side of the ridge, away to the west, was the looming mass of Ben Aldui.

The sun was rising behind them and it illuminated the hillside above as it cleared the shadow of the ridge on the other side of the glen. Copper gold new day above, indigo night below, a line of day slowly creeping down the heather slope. Ian squinted a little and then he saw them, sharply etched on the hillside so far away, the twin shadows that he and Scott were casting.

They lingered there for ten minutes or so, saying little. This was their habit; they had stood in the dawn light and watched their own shadows creep down the far hillside so often that it had become habitual, though still thrilling nonetheless.

'D'ye mind the first time we came here – all those years ago?' asked Ian, in a voice that let his listener know that the questioner did not need a reply, that the comment was just an invitation to talk, if he so desired.

Scott smiled slowly, his lips drawing back over the long teeth that had grown longer over the years. 'Aye,' he nodded. But he did not pursue the subject.

Ian tried again. 'It was just like this; the sun, the shadow over there.' He faltered, then took up again. 'Mind, I was less tired then. That slope gets steeper every time, I swear.'

Scott laughed readily now, glad of the change of tack. 'Aye,' he said, nodding. 'Or maybe they just put on a couple of extra feet when we're not here. Send up a couple of lads from the Council, you know.' How sweet the relief of idle chit-chat that did not turn over any untoward stones, he might as well have said.

Ian, now, did not pursue the conversation. He stooped to pick up the rucksack, but Scott politely but firmly took it from him and shouldered it himself. Nothing was said nor needed to be, for this was the routine. The man without the rucksack led, for it was easier for him to pick his way, and so Ian, this time, led off, striking more or less directly along the saddle of the ridge.

The slope here was much more gentle, although the mountaintop that they now were heading towards was still over a thousand feet above them. It was not a great peak, this. No bagger of the Munros would bother with this little outcrop, a mere 2,800 feet high. But it had other significance, on this most significant of days. After all, was this not the first that they had climbed together?

Ian cast his mind back as his body found the relaxed rhythm that he knew would make the climb easy. Yes, so many years ago, now, on whim, they had come, piled into Ian's ancient Jaguar. They had driven through the night, from a party, because a girl – Ian could no longer remember her name, though he could clearly remember her face, eager and round and surrounded by golden ringlets – had said that they should see the dawn from the slopes of Ben Aldui. It was the kind of idea that takes the heart when you're twenty, at a boring student party in Edinburgh. And in any case, Ian had his eye on that particular girl.

And naturally, the others had to come too – no way out of that. The three friends, the flatmates, the inseparables…So it was into the old Jag, with its curious aroma of petrol and leather and mouse urine, and away.

Of course, they'd arrived too late for the dawn: night in the summer is short here. And the girls – because, that was right, Ian's girl had had a friend, thin and quiet with long dark hair, who had nestled in the back between the other two lads, while Ian's girl fell asleep in the crook of his arm, curled up on the bench seat – had been too tired to actually get out of the car to walk up the hill when they got there. Not, thought Ian on reflection, that their party shoes would have stood the first hundred yards.

So they had left the two girls huddled up together under their jackets like sweet-smelling piles of laundry. Ian let himself linger over that memory; the softness and warmth of the girl, the moistness of her skin, the slight and sensual aroma of her sweat and her breath and her sex…And then they had climbed the path up that killer 600 foot slope until they had crested the rise. The sight of that great granite whaleback in the distance had been far too intimidating, to heads just blown clear of hangovers, so they had just climbed this lesser, subordinate peak and then returned to the car and the sleepy girls with their smudged mascara.

*Scurr scurr scurr!* Ian's heart stopped as a grouse burst from the heather not ten feet in front of him, angrily shouting its rebuke at the top of its voice. And now here they were again, swinging their way up this long easy slope. How long since they had done this together? Many years. Ian thought of turning to Scott and asking him the question outright, but the mood now seemed to be for silence and reflection, not chatter. Time for that later.

Well, that first climb together had settled them into it right enough. The bug had bit. Ian, Scott and Tom. Suddenly they were inspired. Together they set about climbing Scotland's mountains. One after the other the Munros had fallen to them.

Somewhere early on the girls (Kate, that was her name – Kate, and Lucy was her friend, thought Ian) became disaffected. Their bags and make-up and toiletries, which had quickly enough moved into the flat at Marchmont Crescent, soon disappeared again. The romance of it had gone, and to be honest, they were much more interested in parties and clubs than getting up in the middle of the night to go and climb some hill they had never even heard of. So it became the three boys again, and though they met other girls, from then on it was always just the three of them who climbed.


Tom, the American, had chosen to study in Edinburgh because of some long distant family connection. He came from upstate New York, he always said. He was fiercely proud of the 'upstate' bit, too, and his brows would furrow if a stranger made the inference that he came from that city of the same name.

After graduation, Tom had stayed on in Scotland to do his doctorate, but then he'd gone back to the States. His family needed him, he said, and he could put them off no longer. It had always been planned that way, he said. That was how it was in his family. So Ian and Scott had called up some of his friends and together they had put him on a plane and waved goodbye; and then away he was gone over the sea, back to the family business and all that was expected of him.

Being so distant had made it difficult of course, but he always tried to come back to Scotland, once a year, even if it was just for a week. Ian and Scott would take their holiday then too, and that way they would get a couple more of the Munros checked off the list. But as the years passed, once a year had become once every two, then three, and latterly even less.

Scott had travelled too. Footloose, he was, cursed with the wanderlust that would never let him bide still, never let him gather the moss; always hungry for something new, yet when he got there yearning for the soft voices and fresh-washed colours of his native land. It was a curse, that, and no mistake.

Ian remembered Scott's wedding; how beautiful it had been. He shook his head. He had always liked Jill, Scott's wife, and he knew that Scott could be difficult – a real loner. More difficult too for Jill, for she was an English girl. The queer moods and desires of her Scottish husband were a mystery to her, hard though she tried to understand and adapt. It was that silence, that distance that killed, that worked like a corrosive acid on the fabric of love, eating at the bonds that made two people come together.

It was like that now, Ian thought, swinging up this hillside. There was Scott behind him, only six feet away, yet insulated from the world – and Ian – by that distance that he wore so easily. He had not always been like that, Ian remembered. In the beginning he had been shy, but not distant. Now he was distant. There was no other word for it. Ian and Jill had become good friends and he knew her well enough to know that at the end, that distance was what had killed the marriage.

She was frozen out into the cold, and the arms of another man, in the end, bitterly crying over a lost love. Jill needed to be involved, needed to be needed; passion was her thing, and the rejection implicit in Scott's distance had been unbearable for her. Ian, who had listened to Jill's remorse in that quiet way of his, knew it. Scott had never remarried, though Jill had and, in doing so, had passed out of their lives.

Ian had always lived in Scotland; like many Scots he could see no purpose or delight or reason in living anywhere else, and so had never found the need. Soon enough he had found a girl who stuck with him. He had married this girl, who bore his children, now grown and at University themselves, and he still had his girl, who had so long before become his wife.

That was the way of it with Ian; he was the stable one, perhaps. Maybe he was dull – sometimes he thought that other people thought he was dull, but then, it was a price he was prepared to pay. Or perhaps he was simply one who recognised his own bounds and did not seek to torment himself in the pointless stretching of them. Certainly it had always fallen to Ian to be the organiser, who tried to get the other two in the same place long enough to tackle a mountain. And the production of children, the following of career, the building of a life, had kept him busy enough to have let the years roll by unremarked.

Now the two men were approaching the top of Ben Aldui. It was a rolling crest, with no defined summit, just a few knolls that were higher than the rest of its rounded whaleback. It was time to break out the biscuits and take a breather. The sun was high enough in the sky to bring real warmth, and the day began to elaborate on its early promise. Ian went to the side of a low outcrop of rock, and Scott swung off the rucksack.

Ian undid the straps and began to rummage inside. Biscuits, coffee. Just right to break their fast. As he felt in the rucksack, unthinking, drinking in the glorious view away down over the glen towards the plain of Strathmore and the distant smoky sea beyond, his hand fell carelessly on the package – that package – and a chill struck his heart.

Ah, yes, *that* package...And how could he have forgotten? It was why they were there, after all; it was what had brought them. He looked round and he saw that Scott was watching him intently, with an expression – well, an expression that Ian could not understand, yet was troubling to him all the same. He glanced away quickly and the brief contact was lost, but Ian knew that for that rare brief instant he had penetrated the walls of Scott's isolation, and had seen a terrible pain deep in his soul.

But that momentary contact made the distance between them greater with its passing, he soon discovered. The biscuits seemed as dry as old bones in his mouth, and not a word passed between the two men. The magnificent view that the bright sun above illuminated below their feet was a welcome distraction t from the yawning chasm that had opened between the two men.

Suddenly Ian shook himself from a reverie of thoughts that were too uncomfortable to entertain any longer. 'Come on,' he said, trying to mask the thickness in his voice. 'It's not far now. Let's make a push for it.'

And so they set off again, swinging up the long slow path. The sweat had began to bead on Ian's brow from the heat and exertion, and the increasing warmth of the morning had wakened the flies that lived in the heather, with the result that his head was surrounded by a small buzzing swarm of dedicated pests.

They did not seem to bother Scott, he noted...So did that distance insulate him from the immediate annoyances of life, too? Or was there something else – Ian stopped, stooped, broke off a sprig of heather for a swat and began to swish at the flies. It had little effect – these were Highland flies – but it gave him something to do, something to occupy his mind, something to force out the dark thoughts that were so close to breaking in to his consciousness, despite his efforts to hold them back.

So, on they trudged, until at last, sweating and their chests heaving, they reached the destination, a great bald rock outcrop that formed the summit of the ridge.

To their left the drop was a sheer three hundred feet drop into the corrie below, and to their right, a steep heather slope. Away over the corrie they could see the glen they had driven up and down the dizzy slope to the right, the little village of Auchdui, with its white-painted hotel, like a model on a toy railway, pretendy smoke rising from its miniature chimneys.

Scott sat down at the edge of the cliff and Ian sat down with a bump beside him. Scott was looking away across the glen and Ian saw that his face was wet, but not with sweat. He realised in the moment of that realisation that his own eyes were moist, and suddenly he could hold back the long-resisted tears no longer and out they flooded, streaming down his cheeks, his body shaking with little sobs.

Again he looked at his companion and saw that he was looking back, and that the floodgates of his being had opened, and all those thoughts he had struggled to hold at bay were now rushing in on him. Ian realised that the awful distance that had so isolated Scott had gone, completely, at least for now, and that he was as open and as innocent and free as he had been so long before.

'It's time. We must do it now,' gasped Scott at last, standing up. Ian slipped off the rucksack and opened it, his hands shaking terribly. There it was – the package, the precious cargo that had come so far, which they, its final guardians, had toiled and sweated this morning to bring to its destination. Clumsy fingers opened the brown wrapping, tore the cardboard packing as they tugged at it, until there, suddenly, before his eyes Ian saw the dread little box, the tiny wooden casket.

'My God, it's so small!' he exclaimed and then could have kicked himself.

But Scott only said, 'What measure of a man is that, then?' seemingly to himself. 'Surely he is measured in other ways.' Then he shook, as if struggling with himself. 'Let's do it, he said, firmly.

'How?' asked Ian. He had not thought out the details, and with his emotions storming round him now like a hellish January gale he could not.

'Together,' said Scott. 'We must both do it together. Tom would have wanted it that way.'

Ian stood up and now he realised that a strong wind had got up, blowing from behind them, over the edge of the cliff. He had to brace himself a little, but he was glad of the breeze, which kept most of the flies away from his tear-soaked face.

The two men stood at the edge of the sheer drop, face to face. They took the little box between them. Ian looked suddenly into Scott's eyes, his own eyes frank and beseeching.

'Should we say anything?'

Scott looked at him quizzically. 'What could we possibly say?' he asked.

Ian shook his head. 'We – *I* – have to say *something.*' He cast about in his mind for some quote, something weighty oration that would be fit to serve the occasion; but none did he find, and was almost in despair when he remembered – the letter!

With shaking hand he fumbled into his inner pocket for it. He had meant to show it to Scott long before, when they first had met down at the car-park, but he had not, and he did not know why. But now was the time. As if it had chosen itself – or as if someone else had chosen it. His trembling fingers found the lavender-scented envelope and he pulled it out clumsily.

'This – this is the letter I got from Tom's mother,' he said, struggling to control his emotions, which were running so high now that he could barely speak. 'The one where she asked if we would – well, you know. Anyway, I'm going to read it now.' Ian brought his feelings under control with a mighty effort of will and, without waiting for Scott's approval, started to read.


*My dearest Ian,*


*Though we have never met, I feel that I know you so well. My beloved son, your friend Tom, passed away yesterday, after a long and terrible illness.*

*They say that the worst thing a parent can do is to outlive their children, and this is the unhappy state I find myself in now. Marcus, my first-born, left us in some stinking swamp far away, and his name is now engraved on that black wall erected by the country he so loved – enough to give his life; Steven, my second, never really recovered from his brother's death and died not long after in a motorcycle accident.*

*And now I have lost Tom, my dear little Tommy who gave up so much to be at my side.*

*No-one knows – nor will they ever – the torture I have suffered over these dreadful last few months, as I watched that awful disease slowly consume my little boy. There are many who would shun him for the path he walked in his life, but I don't, for I knew his great generosity, his ability to give love, his patience, his loyalty; I knew that the sun itself lit his soul from within. I know that you knew him in this way too, and that is why I beg this favour of you.*

*It was his last wish that his ashes should be scattered over the soil of the Scotland he so loved; sad though I am to make this final parting, I must do so, for he was my boy, and this was his wish. There is no-one else whom I could ask but you to perform this commission – this favour – for us; I am too old and too racked by the sadness I have felt to make that journey, and anyway I don't trust myself to let him go. I must stay here with my memories.*

*So I ask you, his friend; will you help him make his last journey? It would mean so much to us all to know that Tom was at rest there, in Scotland, as he wished.*

*It must be such a beautiful place, to have taken my son's heart as it did. He spoke of it so often I have a picture of it with me always, here in my mind's eye, and as long as I live I will forever see my Tommy striding through the heather.*


*God Bless you*


*Ann Macintyre.*


Ian finished the letter, his voice already cracked, his chest heaving. He looked at Scott keenly. He had to ask. It was the question he had wanted to ask all morning, and it had to be asked now, or forever fester in the dark places of his soul.

'Did you know that Tom was – was gay?'

Scott nodded. 'I knew. He and I were close – closer than even you realise, Ian. Poor Jill, she never understood.' He struggled to find words and Ian could see the pain on his face. 'Ach, Ian, you've always been so firm, so sure, following a path that you set out long before – but we're not all like that, and Tom, well, Tom took another path, and there was a time…A time he asked me to take it with him.'

Silence fell for a long moment and then Scott resumed his confession, for that was what it was. 'But I never could. I couldn't bring myself to do it.' He broke off again, and Ian thought that he would continue no more, but then his friend spoke again, his voice harder, and was there an underlay of bitterness in his tones? Bitterness for something lost that could never, now, be regained?

'Dignity and decorum, that's what my father always said, "Dignity and decorum, make them your staff and your buckler, and never put them aside." And he was right; except…Except of course that there's more to life than that, and without the rest, life's a mean sort of a thing…Maybe it would just be better to grab what's offered and think less…*Care* less what others might think… Maybe I gave up my chance of happiness for the sake of approval from a dead father who cared more about what his neighbours thought than about his sons, but I'll never know…Anyway, Tom went back to the States and now he's dead.

'It's too late – it's just too late to think on all of that,' he went on, his tone set and final, the distance he held between himself and others suddenly obvious again. He shook himself. 'What's past is past, and we'll not live our days again for crying over them. We're here to do a job, Ian. Let's do it. Now. If we don't do it now I'm sure I'll not be able to.'


With that he pulled off the lid of the little casket with one hand and with the other jerked it up into the air, Ian's hand following. A grey cloud of the ashes that had been held within swirled around them for a moment and then stretched up into the air. For a fleeting moment as it swirled up like some desert djinn, it formed itself into a figure, a great figure, the figure of their old friend, and he was smiling down at them, one arm stretched out to each of them in farewell, his hands resting on their shoulders.

'Goodbye, Tom,' Ian sobbed, his eyes wide in amazement at the vision he beheld before him. 'Goodbye.'

'That's more the measure of the Tom I knew,' gasped Scott, tears streaming down his face. 'Mighty, aye, mighty. Goodbye, Tom. Farewell – my friend.'

And at that the figure swirled, turned, saluted one last time, formed itself into convoluted shapes, and then whispered away into nothing. Scott and Ian were left alone on the cliff-top with the soughing wind and the clucking grouse and the distant mournful bleating of the sheep.

They turned to face each other and without asking, both realised that each had seen the same thing, seen the ashes form into the image of Tom, seen him reach out, smile, and wave in parting; that they each had heard his voice, thanking them and bidding farewell; that they both knew for certain that his living essence had been there, as utterly and completely impossible as that was; and more, that they felt themselves flooded with the unstinting and undemanding love of their old friend.

They hugged each other on the dizzy cliff-edge and cried for many minutes, each going over in his own mind his cluttered memories, the depth of his loss. Somehow the years of increasing isolation, of distance, the crust of age, washed away from them, and they were for a time as they had been long before, young and innocent and open and free.

Then, in silence, and closer than they had been for a decade, more, even, they turned away. Scott, without thinking, shouldered the rucksack, and they became Ian and Scott again.


Two thousand feet below them they could see the tiny toy hotel at the bottom of that steep slope. Scott drew up short and Ian looked at him in query.

'Shall we?' asked Scott, smiling. Ian looked down – it was a long slope, near twelve hundred feet before the first of the trees, and thick with heather – it would be foolish, irresponsible; the sort of thing that daft teenagers did, not men in stone-shy of sixty. But he too was taken with the madness that had so recently touched them, and closer to God did he feel than ever before – God or whatever power it was that lived unseen all around him and which, for most of his life, he had ignored.

Suddenly he grinned through the tears that still glistened on his cheeks. 'Tom would,' he said simply, laughing. 'Tom certainly would – and anyway, he'll look after us.'

And without further word the two men threw themselves down that unwalked slope, leaping great moonstrides through the quivering dusty heather, scattering all before them, heedless of the shrieking grouse, roaring and laughing and crying all at once.

*During the late 1980 and 1990s I worked as a photographer and journalist across the UK but mostly in and around Edinburgh. One of the most distressing stories that I had to cover – and all too often – was the scourge of AIDS, which is caused by infection with the Human Immunodeficiency Virus (HIV).*

*In the 1990s this horrible affliction became focussed on the city's council housing schemes where youth unemployment was high and intravenous drug use commonplace. But in the first phase of the outbreak the victims were mainly young men from Edinburgh's gay community. I knew many of them, from my time at Art School, so covering this tragedy was just heartbreaking.*

*This story is in memory of all those who suffered.*

# *Jane Birse*

No one who knew her could possibly have thought that Jane Birse was overly given to imagination. Small and plump, with rosy cheeks and slightly gappy teeth, she wore for pleasure and convenience tweed suits, usually with trousers, as she preferred to hide her legs.

She had studied hard at school, and then just as hard at university, before gaining her degree in Law; then she had worked assiduously in practising that which she had learned. Through time she rose to a senior partnership in the firm in which she had served her apprenticeship, a small company of lawyers dealing in mundane matters in a market town where little out of the ordinary ever happened, and when it did, it was enough to warrant months of comment.

Jane married a young man she had met at university. She had brought up a fine family of three, rosy cheeked and open-hearted like herself. At weekends she liked to walk – she lived in an old farmhouse in the country and there were many pleasant walks nearby – with her retriever, a soul as amiable and thoroughly content with life as his mistress.

This then was the life of Jane Birse, forty-five years old: a pleasant husband, a fine family and a comfortable life. Never once had she aspired to the pinnacles of her profession, nor to outstanding success in any part of her life. Jane Birse was a woman who was keenly aware of her abilities and her limitations; she knew what she could achieve and how to, without sacrificing all else that she did. She shared out her life and served it up to family, firm, and herself; they were all quite happy with that, and so was she.

As I said, no-one would ever accuse her of having an excess of imagination; but then, they would not know a little story about Jane that she always kept to herself, buried in the deepness of her memory and close to her heart.

Once, when Jane was much younger, she had not been quite so stocky and solid; her face had not been so round and her hair not so sensibly cut. Once, although even those who had known her then were inclined to forget this, Jane had been petite and pretty in a calm, quiet sort of way. But this young Jane had once stepped outside of the bounds of her carefully mapped out life.

When Jane first went up to university, she met a man there, a tutor, who stole her heart. He was small and lithe, with a short beard and the first trace of a widow's peak; he had brown skin and dancing blue eyes, and a way with words that charmed her soul and inflamed her heart.

Entirely despite herself and her own better sense, she lost no time at all in falling in love with this man. There followed a period of the most ecstatic brilliance, as Jane explored, at the hands of an experienced teacher, all the passion and desire that a man and a woman can share. Every moment that he could steal away – for he was a married man – she spent in the embrace of her lover; every part of his body did she explore, and willingly did she assist him in the exploration of hers.

But Jane even then was no breaker of marriages. She had her pride and she believed that either the thing would come to an end, or she would be embroiled in all the sordid business that surrounds a divorce. For it was characteristic of Jane, and remains so, that she trusted everyone, and ascribed to them the moral standards that she lived her life by.

It never occurred to her, at least not then, at the age eighteen and a half, that this man, with whom she had fallen totally in love, might have played the same game more than once, with a shy but pretty student. At the same time she despised herself for having crossed the line, for having broken that moral code herself.

Jane always loved to walk, and one hot weekend near the end of the summer term, she took herself up the glen behind her parents' little farm with a pad of notepaper and a pen.

With the blue hills all around her and the larks skirling madly above, the warm sun of June warming her and lighting her hair like gold, Jane found herself a hollow behind a heathery tussock. There she was sheltered from the slight breeze that was chilled from the snow that still lay on the high slopes. She snuggled down with her knees tucked up and she began to write a letter to her lover.

She explained that she must bring the affair to an end and that they could never again share a sweet afternoon of love. Just to make sure that she did not fall to temptation, for she did not trust herself, she said that she would not be returning to her studies at the university. She would turn her back on that which she had thought to be her future.

Many bitter tears did she cry as she wrote, her neat schoolgirl hand forming the words in even lines. Her letter was no masterpiece of the literary art; it was just the honest and decent testimony of an honest and decent girl.

She knew that she had eaten forbidden fruit, had seen inside herself the dark passionate soul that lay deeply buried there. She believed that her passion had risen up to destroy her, all her plans, her desires, her work, to shame her and her family; and she was determined there and then to banish the demon forever.

When she had finished writing, she folded up the pages, here and there smudged by tears for an innocence now gone, a hoped-for life that she had just consigned to the oblivion of might-have-been. She shook herself, placed them in an envelope and sealed it, the last touch of her tongue on the gum long and lingering, a reminder of the lover's kisses she had known.

The sun had already set over the western rim of the glen, and the long shadows had deepened into blue. There had risen a slight misty haze over the tops that reached down long tendrils. Jane – whose outpouring had bared her soul and tested her to the limit of her mettle – saw everything etched in brilliant colours, as if a veil had been dropped from her eyes. Every one of her nerves seemed to tingle with life and she could feel all around her the flow, the great tide of Life itself. She felt herself to be open, a blank slate, directionless perhaps; what would the world throw at her now?

She got herself up and threw her flask into her little rucksack, taking care to tidy up the place where she had poured out her heart to her lover (who even as she wrote was dallying with another, a brunette, for he liked variety,) and set off across the floor of the glen. She wanted to climb a hill, that rose before her like a broaching whale, on the other side. She knew that from the summit she could look out over the plateau and see the sun descend into the west.

When she arrived at the top she was rewarded by a sight more astonishing than any she had even imagined; lit from behind by the glowing last embers of the sun, a herd of red deer stood not twenty yards away, the closest a stag with mighty antlers.

The deer stood and stared at Jane just long enough for her mind's eye to register this scene, that she might carry it with her always. Keeping perfectly still, she gazed at the deer, the sun, the perfect sky, the white flashes of snow. And then the stag snorted, turned and ran, and all the herd with him. At that moment the sun dipped finally beyond the far hills.

Jane, her heart flooded full and her mind in a dwam, turned her back to the sunset and wandered along the ridge towards a path that she knew she would strike. It was old drovers' road that would take her down though a little cleft in the hilly rampart, through a small wood, down to the bottom of the glen, whence she would make her way home.


Now Jane Birse was at this moment more open, more receptive, than she had ever been in all her young life. The day had been a violent storm of emotions and she was drained; and the vision of loveliness she had just experienced had taken her further. Perhaps the state of mind that she found herself in is enough to explain the events that overtook her next; but Jane herself never believed that it did.

The gloaming was creeping up quickly by the time she struck the old drovers' road; though long since disused for its original purpose, the path was still clearly marked by the feet of the many walkers who used it.

It was here that Jane had the first sensation of something odd. She still felt that she walked in a world of crystal and, suddenly, within the greater sounds of the evening, she thought she could hear a piper, far away. At first she thought it was fancy, but there it was again, drifting on the eddying wind, a piper, unmistakably, playing a lament, long and slow and soulful, but somehow chilling, too.

Jane wondered at this; she had often used this path, which she knew was the quickest and surest way home. Indeed she had so often passed along it that she trusted herself to walk there in pitch dark, if necessary. But she had never, ever heard a piper there before.

And those pipes were getting closer.

Another odd sensation crept over Jane as she walked on. It was that the air blew alternately warm and balmy, which is what she expected after such a glorious day, and freezing cold, as if blowing straight from the coldest of icefields.

Well, in the Grampian mountains of Scotland, patches of ice and snow can persist throughout the summer, so she thought little enough of it; except – except that the sounds of piping were at their most audible when the wind blew that heart-shivering cold. And there was something else; as the cold wind blew, Jane felt herself suddenly fatigued, as if some weird tiredness swept through her limbs.

She told herself, in her practical way, that perhaps she had sat in the sun too long and had caught a touch of heat-stroke – easy enough to do in the mountains. Whatever, it did not seem at first serious.

Then she became aware of another strange thing. She thought, each time that this cold wind blew, and increasingly, that she could smell a terrible odour of decay wafting with it. Now often enough a lost sheep will die out on the hill in winter and lie frozen until early summer and decompose then, which might account for the stench; but there was something else – a dreadful, acrid, burning smell that almost made her eyes water. And this too, was getting stronger, and coming from behind her. Even though she walked as quickly as she dared, she could not match the pace of the approaching piper, and all the queer sensations that appeared to surround him.

She had to take hold of herself, saying, 'Here, Jane, don't be silly! It's just a summer evening, there's nothing to fear!'

At last she came into the woods at the bottom of the cleft in the hills. All at once a great draught of the dread cold air enveloped her. She was so weakened by it that she had to catch hold of a branch, for she felt that she might fall down.

'Now, Jane, this is a silly thing,' she scolded herself again. And as she did so, she recognised something that her mind had blotted out till that moment. She could hear the sounds of footsteps.

Behind her, approaching quickly, people were following. Their gait was curiously unhurried, almost shuffling, but despite that, the unseen walkers were moving with relentless speed. She knew at once that there was not one but many; and she soon made out the quiet murmur of voices.

Usually she would have been happy enough to fall in with a band of walkers taking the same path as she, but with a certainty that she could never have explained, she knew that this was a group to be avoided. Not even feared; dreaded.

Jane Birse, aged eighteen and a half, suddenly knew what it was to feel real terror mount in her gorge, and she hurried on as quickly as she could in the dark, her breath rasping.

Few things can be as frightening to a woman as to be fleeing along a rough path in the near dark, through the impenetrable shadows of a wood, with the steps of something terrifying coming up quickly from behind. And worse, each time that the cold wind blew, she felt the life-force sucked from her, until at each exhalation of its poisoned breath she staggered; and those gusts came more and more often, until she could hardly walk.

At last, tears of fear streaming down her face, weakened by the weird effect of this terrible cold wind that stank of corruption and brought the sounds of those who followed her ever closer and closer, Jane Birse realised that she could not outrun them. Instead she must turn to face what she feared.

The place was a widening of the path, not quite a clearing, a little blair in the forest where the ground plants grew thick. Jane was glad of the scent of the wild garlic crushed under her feet, which helped to suppress the awful stench.

Then they – the followers – came into view, and Jane Birse paled to her roots and her knees almost gave way in fright. No party of mortal walkers was approaching along the path she had just hurried along, but the faintest outlines of a number of men, twenty-five or perhaps thirty in all.

They were all young, about her age, and they were dressed strangely, in dark suits, white collarless shirts, and flat caps. Each carried, either on his shoulder or in his hand, a grey blanket bundle. Their boots – which were nailed – struck harsh on the path, but the sound seemed much more distant than the feet that caused it. Although it was quite dark under the trees, she could see the men clearly, as if they were lit by some luminescence they carried with them.

Jane was transfixed with horror as the monstrous apparition bore down upon her. She stood in the centre of the road, which was wide at this point. She was unable to move.

The infernal dirge of the piper still shrilled on, the low rumble of speech surrounded her, and she nearly choked at the ghastly stink, from which there was no longer any relief. But the eyes, the eyes were the worst – their dead light rooted Jane to the spot and split her aching heart in two.

These were the eyes of dead men, she realised; but worse, in them was written the tale of dreams unfulfilled, hopes dashed, hearts broken, lives sundered. Jane's whole body shuddered in all-consuming terror, her heart pounded against her ribs, her eyes stared open.

But then a strange thing happened. She realised with a flash of insight that she had nothing to fear from these terrible walkers, that they sought not to harm her; that it was simply – simply that *they walked the same path.* And somehow, in that instant, she also realised that they were condemned to do this, carrying their dreadful burden of sorrow, for ever.

Then her heart went out to these young men, whoever they were; she felt the tears – not of fear now, but of compassion, run down her cheeks as they came closer and closer. Though she found herself quite incapable of speech, she reached out her hands to them.

They did not stop, but passed her by and, with the passing of each she felt a kind of sigh, a waft of wholesome breath lost amongst the foetid stench of the grave – for that, she now realised, was what assaulted her so.

On and on they passed, each one gliding by on unseen, though quite audible feet; each one staring with dead eyes full of loss straight through Jane and beyond her, each one passing her by as delicately as a horse might pass a child.

Until the last, that is. He came straight at Jane and did not deviate, not one measure. She felt sure that he would pass right through her and braced herself, still unable to move, for this most unwelcome of experiences.

But no. At the last the apparition stopped. He stood before Jane, and took off his cap and put it in the pocket of his jacket. She could see that he was tall, with short cropped black hair, and handsome, with the reddened cheeks of the man who has spent his days outdoors. He stood before Jane for what seemed an age and then he raised his hands and took hers, which were still outstretched.

At once Jane's sobs became louder as she felt all the pain of parting, of love forever sundered, of hearts broken and wasted lives; she felt Loss through those phantom hands.

The man – or boy, for she could not tell his age, his form seeming to change itself subtly before her eyes, looked deep into her soul. And then he leaned forward and gently brushed his dead lips against hers, and somehow she knew – somehow the man *told* her – that she must close her eyes and keep them so.

As she did as he commanded she was struck by a terrible burning, choking sensation that seemed to consume her. She did not know how long this impression lasted, but she knew that some deadly mist seemed to swirl around her, some horrible expression of great evil, feeling clammy on her skin, and the one thing, she was quite sure, that protected her, was the light touch of the phantom hands that held hers.

At the same time she felt that somehow the man was talking to her, but not in words that she could hear; he seemed to be speaking inside her head. And his words were strange, like the half remembered speech of dreams, that makes no sense yet which we know has meaning. He was telling her something, and oh, if only she could understand what it was...

Then, as quickly as it had begun, the terrible choking, tightening sensation passed, and at that the ghostly hands slipped from hers.

Jane opened her eyes again and found that she stood alone in the darkened clearing. The first stars twinkled over her head, and the balmy June air was full of the scent of new mown hay, flowering heather, wild garlic and the aroma of peat smoke from some distant hearth. Tendrils of honest Scottish mist licked around the trees, but of handsome young men with pale dead faces and haunting eyes she saw nothing, nor of the cloud of fear that followed them; even the piper had ceased his heart-rending dirge, and all she could hear now was the sad mewling of a lonely whaup.

Jane made her way down the path, at first with trepidation, but soon with confidence. She had the distinct impression that some-one unseen walked beside her, someone not to be feared, someone who would protect her. She could no longer see him and every other queer sign had passed, yet she knew that the young man walked beside her, helping her on her way, though silently and invisibly now.

At the end of the wood the path opens out into a broad meadow before it joins the tarmac road. As Jane left the shelter of the trees she felt the slow passing of the unseen presence, until, as she approached the village and its lights, she was aware – feeling rather than hearing – of a deep sigh, distant, lingering and full of longing, and then she was once more truly alone.

Jane knew that she must stop at the inn, because she was much later than she had planned, and she knew that her parents would worry; so, sensible girl that she was, she went in to use the phone.

The bar was almost empty, and the barman smiled as she entered. She ordered a shandy – she was not much of a one for the strong drink – and chatted to him for a while. He asked where she had been till this hour of the night, and she explained, leaving out the more interesting detail of her uncanny experience.

When the barman went about his work Jane became aware that another was in the bar, watching her with an intense gaze. It made her most uncomfortable, until at last the man spoke.

'You saw them, then.' It was not a question. Jane nodded. She knew what he was referring to.

'What – *who* – are they?'

The stranger lit up a cigarette and puffed once or twice, and then he spoke. In 1915, the young men of the high glen had volunteered to fight the Kaiser, he explained. 'They all packed their bundles and walked down the road to Kirriemuir, to the recruiting station, where they took the shilling and signed up. They left families, wives, sweethearts. All gone to fight for King and country.'

'What happened to them?'

'They were all, every one, killed in a gas attack at Ypres, barely a week after they joined the line.'

Jane hung her head and nodded. Then she looked at the stranger again. 'You've seen them, too?' she whispered.

'Oh, aye. The fifth of June, every year, they tramp that cold road of broken hearts. But they don't speak to me.'

'There was one...he touched me.'

'You must have a good and open heart, then. There was one that met his lassie for the last time at the clearing in the wood above the bridge. While the others went on ahead, they walked together, never speaking, till they got to the road. And then the lassie had to go home and the lad went away to war. They never saw each other again, at least not in this world.'

The man paused, a strange light in his eyes.

'He'll have told you something, lass. Heed it. They don't speak but to those that have need, and a wise body listens.'

Jane pondered this. The barman came back to her to ask if she wanted another drink; Jane was about to say no, but perhaps the stranger would. She turned to look again; but he was gone, only the swinging door betraying his exit.

'Never mind Tam,' said the barman. 'He aye has some queer tale. But he's harmless for all that.'

But Jane knew that Tam was telling the truth.

As she rose to leave, she looked at herself in the mirror behind the bar and saw there not the young girl who had left the family home that morning, burning and twisted with passion and shame over a foolish infatuation. Facing her in the dusty reflection instead was a woman, confident and wise.

She realised what the words of the young man – she could not bring herself to think of a presence so real as a ghost – had meant, now.

He had told her that the worst thing that she could do was to give up her dreams; that she must face whatever she must to achieve them; that she must not let her life's ambitions be lost, as the ambitions of those men had been, stricken down by senseless evil, in the foul mud of a faraway trench in France.


She reached into her pocket and pulled out the letter she had spent all day writing. Without opening the envelope, she tore it into little squares and dropped them into the ashtray on the bar.

She would not run away. She would return to face her shame and her guilt, she would be strong and resist temptation; and she would finish that which she had set out to do.

And so she did.


*I wrote the notes that developed into this story in the 1980s after a hot day in Glen Clova. At the end of the afternoon I climbed a hill to the south to watch the sunset. There I was confronted by a herd of red deer. As I walked back down towards the hotel where my car was parked, I had the idea for Jane Birse; but it didn't fully form, because I couldn't see the central character.*

*Some time later I met a woman lawyer who fitted the role perfectly; if she recognises herself I hope she accepts this as a compliment.*

# *The Impression of a Hand*

A few years ago now, I had recently returned from a trip of many months to the East and was even more sensitive to the Scottish climate than is usually the case. I had been back a day and a night and had begun the long task of sorting through the pile of mail that had built up during the months of my absence, when the second post of the day brought the most unwelcome news.

Briefly, my old friend, drinking companion and steadfast ally, with whom I had shared an inordinate number of adventures, was dead, after a serious and unspecified illness.

Hector Morison – for that was his name – was to be buried after a funeral service at the West Kirk in the town of Arbroath, on Thursday morning. The note was unsigned, only initialled, but at once I recognised the scrawling hand of its author.

I was shocked and I remember pacing around the living-room with the note in my hand, reading and re-reading it as though somehow this might make the words change themselves to something less unbearable. A visit to Hector had been the first thing I had planned to do once I had cleared my feet of the humdrum and necessary. He could always be relied upon to have a few bottles of decent Burgundy and was as fine a companion as I ever have known.

So it was with a deep sadness in my heart that I once again packed my bags and prepared to travel; this time to drive the hundred or so miles north from my adopted home of Edinburgh, to Arbroath.

That was where I grew up and where Hector and I had first drunk deep of life. There seemed an ill-boding finality in the solid clunk of the lock, as I closed the door of the Georgian eyrie that had for so long been the closest thing I ever had to a home.

I arrived in Arbroath on Thursday morning after an uneventful journey. I made my way to the Kirk, parked my car and walked the last few yards. Hector had always been a popular man – even amongst his enemies – and the service was well attended.

I slipped to the back of the congregation and found a pew. I need not dwell on the details of the sermon, which was delivered in that peculiar half-sung speech of the Presbyterian clergy. However I remarked certain morbid references to my departed friend's 'recent troubles' in which the word 'torment' figured more than once.

The eulogy was given by Hector's brother Hugh, who was clearly deeply upset. The last months of Hector's life had been difficult and he had suffered some form of illness –  the nature of which remained unexplained. There seemed an inference that this malady had not been entirely of a physical nature. My mind filled with unpleasant and tantalising possibilities, I studied Hugh's face for some greater clue as to what had actually befallen his brother. But nothing in his expression gave any hint at all, save the obvious sadness and shock that he was suffering.

Yes, my imagination was piqued, all right, by a grim and morbid curiosity; you could not have imagined a more down-to-earth, stolid, no-nonsense character than Heck. The suggestion that he had been afflicted at the last by some form of psychological crisis or even madness was shocking. I made up my mind to find out everything there was to know about it, even if it meant imposing on his brother at his hour of grief. I had been a close friend of Hector's since school, after all.

However I was spared the unpleasant task of questioning a man in such distress when, as we filed out of the kirk into the watery gloom that passed for day, I finally caught sight of the man who had initialled the note I had received.

Jim Wilkie was another close friend, and another larger-than-life character. As soon as he saw me he pressed through the crowd and shook my hand earnestly. We exchanged a few words appropriate to the surroundings and then fell silent as the pall-bearers, with gliding step, brought the coffin containing our old friend into the day for the last time.

'Are you going to the kirkyard?' asked Jim. I shook my head and he nodded. 'Neither am I. Nothing left to be said now.' He looked away at the hearse where the coffin was being loaded, where Heck's wife and children, all now adult or nearly so, looked on with tear-streaked faces. 'I'll leave it to them – it's better that way.' He turned his gaze back to me. 'I suppose you'll be needing a few answers, then?'

I nodded grimly and came straight to the point. 'What was all that about Heck's 'trouble'? It wasn't the drink catching up at last, was it?'

Jim shook his head, a light of dark humour in his eyes. 'By rights it should have been, after the life he led, but no, it wasn't. It might have been better if it had been, but Heck's liver was as strong as ever when he died.'

Once again it was there – the hint, the inference, the fact not stated. I had become attuned to it by then.

Jim nodded and sighed. 'They're having a lunch for those who care to attend at the Viewie if you fancy,' he said, in a voice which made it clear that he did not, 'But then we could go down to the Courtyard instead. They do a nice fish there and I booked a table for us; I knew you'd come.'

This was just the kind of forethought that I had come to expect of Jim. I gladly accepted the invitation.


We left our cars and walked to the inn, as the day, though cold and grey, was dry and the sea air was refreshing. We did not once mention Hector or his death as we walked, instead catching up on our personal news. We hadn't seen each other for several years and the opportunity to fill in the gaps was a welcome diversion. It was not until we were wedged into a cosy corner by the fire, our orders taken and our drinks served that he at last opened up.

'Did you know Hector got divorced?'

I had to confess I had not; I had been so long and so often out of the country in recent years that a good deal had passed me by. Jim, on the other hand, had always been happy to make his life in the old town. He had married his girlfriend from school, then worked his way up from cub reporter to editor and then owner of the local newspaper. Thus he had become my conduit of information about events in my home town.

'Aye, it was a messy business, like they always are. I was pleased to see Heather there today, because there was a time she would've throttled Heck. Or he would've throttled her. Anyway, in the end, she got that big house he'd built. That and her shares in the company, was her price, and Hector had to lump it.

'Well, once the dust had settled, Heck went and bought a place over by Friock, at Bolshan. I thought it was a grim hole myself, but he liked it. Maybe it fitted his humour – the split with Heather hit him hard, and not just in the wallet. Anyway, there was a farmhouse with a steading, and a garden. He had the idea that he was going to develop the steading and turn it into a craft centre – you know how he always had some scheme up his sleeve.

'Pretty quickly Heck got the garden set torights – just got a couple of handy lads in to do it. Then he went to work on the house itself. He seemed to have really got his teeth into the project, and I was happy for him. He needed something to kick-start his life after what had happened.

'He used to drop by the office quite a lot at that time; he was taking a less active role in the company, partly because his sons were running it, and partly so he wouldn't see Heather, I think. To tell you the truth he'd been resting on his laurels for a long while and this new project seemed to be just the thing he wanted to put the spring back in his step. We used to come here for lunch and a beer quite regularly, as a matter of fact.

'Whenever we met he was full of his plans for the place at Bolshan. He was convinced it would be a success – he was going to put in all sorts of facilities, let units, have a craft shop and garden centre – well, Heck had a habit of making things like that work out, and he had all the right backers. But it was the house that seemed to interest him most. It was as if it had got under his skin; I couldn't for the life of me think why.' He chuckled. 'You could hardly have had a more unprepossessing place – but he thought it was charming. So it was going to be new this, new that, after the style we all knew and loved (here I smiled wryly) and as usual he was happy to throw money at it.'


'About the end of July last he dropped by, full of the joys. Some deal he'd been quietly working on had paid off. As usual a fair bit was going into that house of his and now he was for putting in the double glazing before the weather turned. Well you couldn't blame him for that. It's a raw blasted hole up there and the windows were a disgrace. You'd have thought it was the paint holding them together.

'I had a chat with him about it and he said a queer thing. I remember, clearly, he said, "Oh, the old windows, they've really had it. The worst of it is the stains. They're all covered in stains and I just can't get rid of them."

'At the time it seemed innocent enough, though I remember thinking that I'd seen a few things in old houses, but not windows having *stains*. But he didn't amplify, so that was that. Pity really.' Jim paused as the waitress brought the first course.

'Anyway, away he went and ordered his windows. To be honest with you that was the last I saw of him for a wee while. It was a busy time ; I had staff shortages and holidays and all sorts of things that I wouldn't trouble a globe-trotter such as yourself with. After a while it died down though and I got back to researching for a book I'm writing on local history.

'I happened to be going through some old stuff at the museum here and I came across a book on Friockheim and the area. Lo and behold, there was a story about Bolshan, and as far as I could work out the location was the farm Heck had taken such a shine to. Well, I knew straight away that was going to have to go into the book I was writing, naturally.

'Grim tale, though, so it was. Apparently there was a great scandal in the 1880's. The farmer who had the place then was known to be a tyrant. He was dangerous with the drink on him. Evil old sod if you ask me. Anyway he had two sons, but they'd both upped and left for soldiering rather than stick it, and his wife had died long before. He just had one daughter left in the house besides himself. Anyway he had forbidden the girl to go out courting. He was so serious about this that he put iron bars on all the downstairs windows and locks on the upstairs for good measure.

'Well, it seems that his daughter was not one to be so easily beaten. She had struck up with a lad from a nearby farm, and they began to meet on the quiet.

'She discovered that her father hadn't bothered to put a lock on one window. This gave out onto the roof of the porch at the front door. The old man obviously didn't think anyone would be able to escape through the narrow opening, and if they did it was hard to see how they would get down from it or up again. Or maybe the old bugger just forgot. Anyway the lass was a clever one and found herself a bit rope, so she could shin up and down to get in and out of the house without being discovered.

'The daughter would wait till the old man was asleep and then slip out of her room, open the window, slip down the rope, rendezvous with her man, and then sneak back in again later.'

'Fairly usual for a teenager, I should say,' I interjected, laughing.

'Aye, and you're not the only one to twig that. Soon the whole parish – except the father of course – got to know what was going on, and the father was a laughing stock. It seems he was roundly detested in the area anyway.

'One day in the dead of January the old man had spent the afternoon boozing at The Station in Friock – a popular watering hole. Well, he had a barney with somebody and as a result of this the tale of his daughter's trickery came out. White as the snow that was falling outside in his rage, the old man made his way back over the hill to Bolshan.

'When he got home the place was engulfed in a terrible snow-storm – you know how it catches it up there. Never a word did he breathe to the lass, but he went to his room and instead of falling asleep he watched and waited. Sure enough, the girl tiptoed out of her room, down the stairs to the landing, opened the little window over the porch, out with the rope hidden there, and away she slips just as you like.

'That old man was an evil bastard. He didn't chase after her and chastise her; no, he'd a better plan to teach her a lesson. He took his tools and he nailed that window up so that never again would anybody be able to open it. He made sure that every one of the other windows and doors was bolted and barred. And then he took himself to his bed and drank whisky until he fell into a stupor.

'By the time the poor daughter got back, the snow had fallen thick and was still falling. It was a bad night to be out, but love, as they say, knows no bounds. Imagine – she gets to her rope, shins up to the window, and instead of being pulled to, she finds it nailed tight shut so she can't open it. Maybe she even saw the nails and realised that somehow her father had found her out. Such was the terror the girl had of her father that instead of going to find her sweetheart and seeking shelter with his family, she rushed round the house time and again trying all the windows and doors. The snow was beaten quite flat by her feet as she went round and round the house, desperately trying to get in from the cold.

'Then, perhaps believing that she could force the little window, perhaps believing that her father would hear her pleas and relent, she climbed back onto the porch. Well, whether she pleaded or not, and whether the old man heard or not, nobody knows; certainly I don't. But the next again morning there was that poor young lass still on the porch roof with a light covering of snow on her. She was as stiff as a board, her outstretched hand literally frozen to the pane of glass, and of course she was quite dead too.

'The body was seen by a passer-by just after first light, and soon the doctor and the constable from Friock arrived to take care of the poor girl. But never a sign of the father was there. Quickly a large and angry crowd, led by the girl's sweetheart, had surrounded the farmhouse. They battered on the door and demanded to see the farmer.

'They tried to pin it on him, but it was never going to stick. He said he hadn't known his daughter was out and that he had forbidden her to leave the house. As far as he knew she was in her bed where she belonged; the window had been banging during the night and he'd nailed it up. And with the wind howling, how could he have heard his daughter's  cries?

'For all that within a year he had sold up and disappeared.

'As an aside it seems that he had been a great brute of a man with wild red hair and beard. But by the time he left, his hair was as white as the snow that his daughter had frozen to death in. I kind of like details like that in a yarn.'

'Well, you see how I couldn't help but think "Now there's a tale," and of course I had to tell it to Heck. You know how he always had a taste for the macabre – loved a good ghost story, he did, and I thought he'd be delighted to hear this one. So I went over to Bolshan to see him.

'When I got there I thought right away that something was up. Heck looked like he hadn't slept in a week. He was unshaven and his red hair was dirty and lank. His skin was grey, and his eyes were yellow and bloodshot. But he was friendly enough, and he had me in for a dram – which I was glad to accept, because Heck always had a couple of nice bottles, you know. So we went inside and I sat down at the kitchen table while he got out the glasses.

'Pretty soon the dram warmed us up and we fell to jawing as we always had. I must say that even though I had been worried about Heck when I had first seen him, I soon forgot my concerns. It seemed that he was having trouble getting somebody to 'do for' him, and he was finding the bachelor lifestyle difficult. That was why the place was needing a tidy up. And he'd got into some bad habits of staying up late and so on, and that accounted, or so it seemed, for the changes in him. I just ticked myself off for worrying myself and relaxed.

'Then I remembered why I had dragged myself out to his lonely, blasted moor. "Oh I must tell you a story I dug up. Would you believe that dread deeds were done in this very house?" said I, and wished I had not right away. You could have heard a pin drop. There was an intolerable silence, and then at last Heck spoke. "What exactly do you mean by that?" he said at last.

'Well, I would have dodged the subject if I could but I'd put my big foot right in it and there was no way I could back out now. So I told him the story of the girl, keeping it as brief and desultory as I could. When I had finished he got up and began to pace up and down the long kitchen floor. He was sheet white and I could swear that he was shaking. He poured himself another belt – and I mean a serious one this time, and knocked it back in one. Then he muttered something that sounded like "Oh, I know all about her."

'Well that got me going, I can tell you! Here was me thinking that I had a good wee yarn to myself, and the first person I tell it to already knows! So I pressed him. And then a strange thing happened – he hesitated and gave me a queer look, as if he was figuring whether he could trust me – me, that had known him thirty years!

'Then he just laughed and said he had meant nothing at all; he might have heard the story somewhere, that was all. Well, I've been turning over stones in this neck of the woods longer than anyone I know and I'd never heard it, so that really got my goat. So I pressed him more – where had he heard the story, who from? Was it the previous owner?

'To cut a long story short I think I finally got it through to him that I was interested in this in a professional sense, and he lightened up a bit and said "Come on, I'll show you something you'll not see again in a hurry," and led me out of the kitchen and up the stairs. Sure enough, just as the story had told, there was a small window looking out over the porch at a landing in the stair. But it was Heck's reaction that held my interest. As we approached the window he seemed to chill, to slow, as if he was forcing himself to go forward.

'He was in front of me but when he turned so that I could see his face I could swear that it was black with – well I can only say dread. He seemed both horrified and entranced by something at the window, and he beckoned me closer. "Look, there! D'you see it? D'you see it"' he hissed, his voice urgent.

'It had already been late in the afternoon when I had arrived and the time had slipped by deceptively quickly. The sun had set and it was quite dark. It was a pleasant clear autumn evening that foretold of a frost in the morning, with only a wee bit cloud hazing the moon, which was about half. I peered hard into the mirk to try to catch a glimpse of whatever the hell it was that Heck could see. Of course I could see nothing at all, and I once again began to wonder about Heck. So I told him all I could see, which was precisely nothing at all, but he just shook his head impatiently and hissed, '"Not outside! On the window!"

'All I could see was a grubby old window with some smudges on it, set in a frame that was just falling apart with rot. I looked harder at the smudges, but they meant nothing. I was about to make a joke along the lines of "If you'd wash your windows more often then I might be able to see something," and to suggest that maybe another wee dram would help, when the moon suddenly blinked out from behind a cloud and shone its pale light directly onto the glass.

'Heck recoiled as if he'd been struck, but I paid him no heed. For there, suddenly revealed in the moonlight, the smudge on the window pane had turned into the perfect print of a human hand, its palm flat on the glass, fingers spread.

'I was absolutely amazed at this trick of the light, which is what I presumed it was, and I pulled out my handkerchief and began to rub at the glass. But this had no effect. The mark must be on the outside, I thought, though it was hard to see how anyone could have put such a mark there. That window was obviously painted up tight shut. It hadn't been opened in decades. But my antics had a weird effect on Heck; he began to laugh, a laugh with no mirth in it at all, laugh and laugh until I thought either he would choke himself or I might just choke him. "Oh, you'll never rub that mark off," he gasped at length, "Not in a hundred years!"

'I didn't think the game was that funny, and I must admit I was pretty snippy with our poor old friend. "Well," I snapped, "If you're that bothered by it, and it won't rub off, then it's easy enough to fix – just change the glass! This is a terrible old piece." That shut him up though, I can tell ye. He went all quiet and grim, and then, slowly, whilst glaring – yes, glaring at me – he rolled up the sleeve on his left arm, to reveal a blood-soaked bandage.

'"Change the glass?" he whispered. "Change the glass? D'you think I've not tried that, Jim?"

'By this time I was definitely beginning to need another dram, and to change the subject I scolded him for being careless – had he his tetanus up to date? Living here alone it was daft to take silly risks. Had he seen a doctor? I insisted that he did and meantime said I thought it would be a good idea to have the whole place re-glazed by professionals. He seemed happy to go along with that idea, although I had the creeping feeling that he was just humouring me.

'Anyway, to get to the point, I hustled him down to the kitchen, made him promise to get the wound on his arm dressed, to sort himself out and generally to act his years and not his shoe size. I got on my way soon after; it was already getting late. To tell the truth I'd had a worse fright than I've had in a long year. I thought, after the life I've led, that I was past being so shocked. I mean I've heard countless ghost stories, every one a sham, or a legend, never a one of them standing up to any kind of real investigation. But this definitely gave me the willies. I needed to think it through. It was a hoax, obviously – but perpetrated by whom? Heck was never a good enough actor to have carried off such a ploy, so was someone hoaxing him? And if so who –  and why? Not Heather; she has her faults, but downright cruelty isn't one of them. It was a poser, all right.'

'All that night my head buzzed as I tossed and turned trying to get to sleep. At last I persuaded myself that I had been mistaken; that the story of the poor girl who died in the snow must have affected me more than I had thought. Faced with the actual window where it had happened and the absolutely weird atmosphere at Bolshan, I had been the victim of auto-suggestion. Heck had obviously heard the story elsewhere and he had allowed himself to fall into the same delusion. Perhaps he had even communicated this to me. I know, it didn't sound great, but it was all I could come up with.

'As  well as that though, I was both angry at Heck and worried about him –  angry that he had played a trick like that –  which is what half of me was convinced it was –  and worried about him for the state of his nerves. There had been no doubt about the stress in him, the darkness that came over him after the incident on the stair-landing. He became, well, fatalist, bleakly accepting, hardly paying me any attention at all. You realise that this was hardly common behaviour for Heck, who was always for taking the bull by the horns.

'However, the next day who should breeze into my office but the man himself, full of apologies for upsetting me. He had taken matters in hand, the glazing company – who had been prevaricating for ages it seemed – were to start work later the same week, ripping out all of the old windows and fitting new. Surely that would see an end to the persistent stains on the old glass. We went for lunch and chatted about happier things, and then we parted.

'That was the beginning of a right roller-coaster, though I didn't know it then; sometimes Heck was just fine, full of the joys, his usual bumptious self, and then I would hear a story about some strange thing that he had done that worried me, or I would see him and be struck by the rapid greying of his hair, or the hollow, hunted look in his eyes.

'To give you an example, about a week after I had visited Bolshan I heard a curious story about the place. A joiner working for the glazing company that was fitting the double-glazing had gashed his hand taking out some of the old glass and ended up dead of blood poisoning. The story was about the safety record of the double-glazing contractor; neither we nor anyone else thought that the place where the accident had *happened* was an issue at all.

'The effect of this on Heck was catastrophic. For a week he refused to answer calls and was apparently incommunicado, locked up in Bolshan Farm. However, I had three weeks in Florida booked and I had no intention of cancelling. That meant it was late in October, near November before I got a chance to call up at his retreat.

'I can tell you, I was shocked. The beginnings of decline that I'd noticed before – the gaunt aspect, the greying, lank hair, and indeed the weight loss – had accelerated to the point that Heck was literally a changed man. His gait had become a timid shuffle – a far cry from the swagger of old. His clothes were stained and grubby and hanging off him. His beard was quite grey and unkempt and he desperately needed a haircut. He was a shade of his former self, if you'll excuse the cliché.'

'I really was most alarmed about his condition. This was not good at all. In fact I was so worried that immediately, without even troubling to ask Heck's permission, I phoned Ian Strachan. You'll know Ian of course, he's been my doctor for years – not to mention golf partner, fishing companion and associate bar-prop from time to time. Anyway I called him. He and I regularly swap favours and I knew he'd turn to, which of course he did, with hardly more than a passing protest. I thought I'd have to butter Heck up to get him to see a doctor – he had a life-long aversion to medics – but no, that was fine. Heck seemed to have lost the will to resist, and that was almost as worrying as his appearance.

'While we were waiting for Ian, I tidied up the house a bit – it really was a mess, believe me. And there was precious little in the fridge or the larder in the way of provisions either; well, that's hardly the Heck I knew.'

Jim paused, his gaze turned to the flickering log fire nearby. Then he turned back to me and his tale. 'I noticed that he'd had the double-glazing finished. But I also noticed that someone – and someone that wasn't a professional either – had fitted extra locks and bolts to the windows. The place was like Fort Knox. I wondered if Heck had been burgled, or what else might have made him ruin – because that was what he had done – the brand new windows, by fitting all this ironmongery.

'Anyway, Ian arrived soon enough and looked over Heck, who was as meek as a puppy. He was as concerned as I was about the general state of affairs at Bolshan Farm. It turned out that Heck was actually registered to another doctor in his practice, so Ian, who lives just the other side of Friock, proposed to transfer Heck to his own list so that he could keep an eye on him. In fact he'd called his colleague, just out of courtesy, before coming over, and she'd said that as far as she knew, Heck was fine, she hadn't seen him for years. Well, after seeing our friend, Ian didn't think he was fine, and told me so.

'I had been in the kitchen while Ian did his stuff on Heck in the lounge. When Ian came through he asked right away if Heck had any relatives in the area. I explained about the divorce and the difficult situation there and he nodded. 'She ought to be told,' he said to me, 'But if the wife's not prepared to do it, someone will have to keep an eye on him. That might fall to you, unless there's anybody else.' I just nodded and asked him what he thought.

'There's not a lot I can do for him,' said Ian. 'He's pretty run down and the weight loss is a worry, but then he says he's hardly been eating. Really he should go in for some tests, but he doesn't seem keen to leave this place. In my view his main problem is that he's suffering from an advanced case of nervous exhaustion.'

'Well, I knew the divorce had got to Heck – but I thought he'd got the worst of it out of his system. Ian agreed, but I could see he was holding something back. Finally he said, "If I could I'd have him taken into the psychiatric hospital at Montrose for observation. But he flatly refuses to consider it and he's neither non-compos nor a danger, so I can't force him. But if you ask me he needs a lot of looking after. Meantime I've given him some sedatives, which should at least get him some sleep – that's often a factor in this sort of thing. Broken sleep patterns lead to further problems that cause more broken sleep and so on."'

'Ian left, promising to drop by when he could and asking me to try to persuade Heck to see a specialist.

'And so began a terrible period of my life. I can hardly believe that it was less than three months ago.'


'I won't go into too much detail, there's no need. But Heck needed somebody's help, and I was the only one around. Under the influence of the sedatives, Heck improved, and as the weeks passed I saw that there was a definite pattern to whatever it was that afflicted him. He would pass from periods of relative calmness and happiness into the depths of what can only be described as paranoia, and then slowly become nearly himself again. I had read a little about manic depression and I became convinced that the divorce had caused this illness in Heck. I was miles off the track, of course, I know that now, but then…

'The worst was that Heck just would not talk about things at all. He simply evaded the subject of anything that concerned his mood and so forth, brushing it off with "Oh, don't worry," or "Look, it's my business," and he could even be quite harsh. If it had been anyone else I would have washed my hands of the whole thing, but it was Heck, and besides, I was convinced that he was ill. Far worse of course, was that I was convinced that I could help. I couldn't, and in the end I didn't. But I didn't know…What I do now.

'I was visiting Bolshan every day. It was taking a lot out of my professional life, because I had to visit during the daylight hours, and you know how few of those we get in winter. Heck, when he was in his paranoid moods, would simply refuse to even come to the door, after dark. And he just would not give me a key. During these paranoid moods, I should explain, he was like a hunted animal, always glancing around him, as if he was afraid of someone – or something.

'However he was never so bad as to be completely out of it, you see. He was always able to do business, and even at his worst, if you'd met him for the first time, you'd have thought he was a pretty strange cove, but you'd not have thought he was mad or anything. It was just that I knew him so well. I knew he was far from right, and so did Ian, but it was nothing we could put the finger on. And as I said, try as I might he would not open up. He just would not talk.

'Something happened early in December that struck me as odd, and which maybe I should have paid more heed to. I arrived at Bolshan one morning to find the local builder there. Heck had asked him to brick up the window above the porch. But there was apparently some problem and he and Heck were having a row about it. It was just like the old Heck, which I was pleased about, though the whole thing was a bit weird.

'It seemed that the builder couldn't get his cement to set or something. Both he and Heck were pretty roused but in the end the builder just walked away. As he passed me I heard him muttering something about there being "some auld hooses that should jist be left tae fa doon." He jumped in his van and away he went in a cloud of blue smoke, promising to come back with some new cement. Which, of course, he never did.

'As it came to Christmas, Heck seemed to improve and I invited him – well, I insisted really – to spend the holiday with me and my family. I didn't relish the thought of driving out every day; the police round here know me well enough, but they're a bit too handy with the breathalysers at that time of year. To my surprise, Heck hardly resisted at all. It was the best I'd seen him for weeks, and I hoped we'd seen the worst of it.'

All over Christmas he was back to his old self, you'd have said. Full of jokes and cheer, always entertaining, just as he had been for so long, great company. He stayed three days with us and I will always remember them.

'Then, just before he was due to leave, I saw that look come back into his eyes. I knew – I thought I knew – what it was, and I tried to persuade him to stay a bit longer. I said he could stay with us until he found another place; that he should sell Bolshan, get shot of it and move into the town where he would be surrounded by his friends. But he only shook his head and he had that stubborn look that told me he wouldn't shift. He had to go back, he said.

'I came down with a bad dose of the 'flu after the New Year – in fact I'm really just over it now – so I had to content myself with phoning Heck most days. I must admit he gave away nothing to suggest that he was in decline again, and I was reassured. I can tell you I felt much better about him than I had since November – Heck looked like he was well on the mend from whatever it was, and that 'flu had knocked me sideways – and to tell the truth, seeing to Heck while he was bad had drained my reserves too.

'Well, anyway, it turns out I shouldn't have been so sanguine. Exactly two weeks after he left, when I was just getting back to fitness, I was wakened one night by the phone ringing. I thought at first that it was something to do with the paper – we'd had a few break-ins and I'm the key-holder – but when I got to the phone the voice I heard set my teeth chattering.

'It wasn't a voice I recognised and it seemed a long way away; but it wasn't crackly like a bad line, just – well, far away. It was a girl's voice and she spoke with a strong accent. Not many folk round here can speak the Scots like that these days. The voice wasn't speaking to me, I should say, it was sort of half-singing, half-chanting, the words to a song. The voice was so distant and faint that I could only make some of it out, but it sounded like one of those old music-hall songs. It certainly wasn't anything modern.

'I tried to persuade myself it was some joker playing a hoax on me but when I look back, I knew who it was at once, and the whole horrible thing was clear in a flash. And then, just to confirm it, I heard Heck's voice, just as distant, calling out "Come back! Come back!" and over it that cracked girl's voice chanting her maddening ditty.

'I was dressed and in my car before I had time to think what I was doing. I called Ian on the mobile phone and, though he was none too pleased to be wakened, he agreed to meet me at Bolshan. I drove like hell and I can tell you, it was a bad enough drive, but a far worse arrival.

'There was no need for me to go looking for Heck. He was lying in the road about a quarter of a mile from the house. There had been a heavy fall of snow, but the sky had cleared. Heck was lying face down in it, dressed only in his nightrobe and pyjamas; his feet were bare. As I ran and knelt beside him I heard another car pull up. It was Ian. He rushed to my side and knelt down too.

' "My God!" he gasped, after feeling for a pulse.

' "We're too late," I said.

'Ian nodded but his face was incredulous as he looked at me. "Man, he's stone cold. It's like he's been lying out here for hours. But it was still snowing when you phoned me – and look – there's not a flake of snow on the body!"

'That moment was bad. I could feel the fear rising in me, so that I had to struggle to fight it back. Then the moon – a full moon – came out and lit up the scene like daylight. It was then that we saw – my God, I didn't realise how hard this would be – we saw that there were *two* sets of footprints in the snow. One set was made by a barefoot man, but the other was made by someone, or some*thing*, much smaller and lighter, wearing a pointed woman's shoe.

'It was also revealed, by that deadly moon, that Heck had been following the other person, because his footprints sometimes crossed over the others. He had been running, as the balls of his feet were deeply imprinted but the heels hardly at all. Both sets of prints ended where Heck lay, with no sign of the others continuing. Let me put that another way. The snow around the body was untouched but for the prints that led to it. You understand?'

I nodded. I confess, the hairs on the back of my neck were standing up.

'Ian snapped me out of the shocked horror that I had fallen into. "I'll call the police," he said. "There's nothing more to be done for him, poor bugger." Ian called them on his mobile and then we made our way towards the farmhouse to wait. We took great care, I assure you, not to tread in those footprints. I really don't know what we expected to find at the house, but what we did find sent another cold chill through me.

'The last bright moonlight before the dawn was shining on the farmhouse and under its silver light I could see that every pane of every window was covered – covered with white marks. From a distance it looked like rime, but of course it was too warm after the snow, and in any case I knew fine what those marks were. After all, I had seen one before. They were hand prints, all made by the same hand, the hand of a girl with a broad palm and short fingers.

'And as we approached the house, both of us silent except for the chattering of our teeth, there was one final, dreadful surprise. The front door was wide open of course, which was only to be expected; nobody runs out into the snow wearing no slippers and troubles to shut the door after themselves.'

'But above the porch we could clearly see that the little window there was hanging wide open too, despite all its locks and bolts.'

*This kernel of this story was first related to me by my colleague Brian Smith, who then worked for The Courier in Dundee. The original location, according to Brian, was somewhere in Aberdeenshire. I relocated it closer to home.*

# *Beware The Shadows*

Dear Mrs Geddes,


Please forgive my writing to you in this unannounced fashion; however, there are pressing circumstances which I must inform you of. I hope that what I have to say will excuse this intrusion.

I enclose a diary, which recounts the last few weeks of the life of your late brother, David Hamilton. At the author's request I have read this diary myself, indeed you might say I have studied it in depth. I beg you to read it in detail yourself, even though this may be difficult for you.

I especially ask that you take particular care over the passages which I have marked. I must urge you not to put this letter aside but to read it at once and to act upon it. I only hope that it has not arrived too late.


My name is Roger Horribine. I was the owner and editor of the Seaforth Chronicle. I doubt if you will ever have heard of this little paper; it occupies itself with the local news in and around the town of Seaforth, in Aberdeenshire.

I was not always a local journalist, however; I have had ink in my blood since I was a boy, and for most of my life I worked in Fleet Street. It was only five years ago that I inherited the Chronicle, on the death of my uncle. I made the decision to move from the city and to spend the rest of my working life in relative calm and comfort, passing my days between the office and the golf course.

I thought I'd never again leave that place; but three months ago I accepted an offer to buy the Chronicle, put my house up for sale and have since moved away from the town.

In my profession I saw many strange things, many unpleasant things, many weird things, and many unnatural things; but I have never seen anything that shook me so profoundly as the events surrounding the death of your brother.

Those tragic and terrible events are now of urgent concern to you. I only hope that I am not too late; for if I can find you, I am certain that *they* can. I am sure that they have methods that I can't conceive of.


I met your brother just under five months ago. He had been sent to Seaforth to investigate some curious prehistoric relics that had been uncovered on the beach.

The local council had commissioned a new sewage treatment plant, and this involved laying a pipe along the beach in front of the town for nearly two miles. While the contractors were digging the last section of the trench they discovered a strange construction buried deep in the sand.

It consisted of a circle of wooden stakes, like a sort of palisade. The timber was blackened and gnarled and it was clearly ancient. Well, naturally work had to be stopped at once to allow this to be investigated.

There was a lot of excitement; I went down to the beach immediately, to take pictures. The council's Historical Officer arrived soon after me, He was able to give me enough to make a story out of it, which I managed to get into that week's edition of our paper.

Work on the pipeline trench was suspended over the weekend and the Council contacted Historic Scotland; and the next Monday morning your brother arrived to take a look. I happened to be at the site when he arrived.

I took to your brother at once. I don't know how long it is since you last saw him, but the David Hamilton I met that day was a dapper little man, balding, with a greying beard. He wore those half-glasses that schoolteachers used to wear, which he balanced on the end of his nose. He was constantly bobbing his head back and forward as he talked to you, first looking through the lenses and then not, so that he gave the impression of a bird pecking at seed.

He was light and energetic in his movements and he was certainly one of life's enthusiasts. He was also a keen golfer. I became fond of him over the next few weeks and so did my wife. He was a charming man and we both miss him a great deal. But I digress.

David examined the site and then asked the Clerk of Works to order further excavation under his control. The Clerk agreed; he was anxious to get on with the job, having already lost several days.

As the site was cleared we saw that there was a full circle of stakes driven into the sand, which was only broken where the contractor's digger had first struck it. This circle was about forty-five feet in diameter.

Once the tops of the stakes had been cleared, David asked the digger operator to go much more slowly, until he had cleared the entire site, so that he could take stock of what was there. At the centre of the circle of stakes, which was more or less complete, was the stump of a huge tree.

All of the wood, though much blackened, was surprisingly well preserved, probably by the salt water and the fact that the sand had excluded the air. Most of the stakes were in good condition, and they all had peculiar markings carved onto them.

The stump itself had similar markings. I had no idea what they were, but David said that they were runes, which was a form of writing the Vikings had used. He was excited about them, and explained that they were an unusual form. This seemed to mean something to him, but at the time I paid scant heed to it.

In any case, David had little time to explain. Every moment that the diggers and lorries stood on the beach added to the already enormous cost of the project. To re-route the sewer around the site was impossible and to carry on excavating the trench for the drain meant destroying it completely. There was nothing for it but to map out the site as accurately as possible and then remove the artefacts for preservation elsewhere.

While this was being discussed between David, the contractor, and the Clerk of Works, I became aware of someone standing at the top of the beach watching us intently. There had been a crowd of onlookers since the discovery was first announced, as there always is at that sort of thing; not much in the way of excitement happens in Seaforth, you know.

They were restrained from entering the site itself by a yellow perimeter tape, so that the nearest was about ten yards from the excavations.

Today there was one in particular who caught my attention. He was a tall, gaunt man, who stared at us with a steady, threatening gaze that I did not like at all. He was apart from the others, pushing forward against the tape. It was stretched tight against his body and he seemed to be talking to himself. I could see his lips moving. He wore a hat and a long dark coat; he was thin, and his collar was turned up, even though the day was sunny and warm.

It was impossible to make out his features, because he had his back to the sun and his wide-brimmed hat cast a shadow over the upper part of his face, but his eyes seemed like two black chips of moonstone, little points of pale light, unblinking and unrelenting. Whereas the rest of the onlookers were chatting and laughing and pointing things out to each other, this man just stared and mumbled, with that black menacing gaze.

He really made me shiver, and I know David didn't like it either; he kept glancing over his shoulder at the man. But there was nothing we could do, as long as he kept on the other side of the tape; the beach is a public place after all.

A decision came after twenty minutes or so of heated debate, during which the contractor made it clear that he had little time for ancient stumps. But the final word was with the Clerk of Works, who, though he sympathised with the contractor, agreed with David that the artefacts had to be preserved.

David would be given time to measure the site and to make accurate drawings, and then the artefacts would be removed and taken to the disused fish-market building at the harbour. There they could be kept covered and soaked in salt water until they could be properly catalogued and transported elsewhere.

The contractor, sighing heavily, stood down his men for another day. Then David was out with his rule and level and his camera and notebook. He took no notice of the rest of us as he went about the job of measuring, photographing and annotating.

I glanced, sometime about then, back up the beach and saw that the tall thin stranger was still staring down with that icy gaze. I thought I'd go and speak to him, to find out what he thought, but as soon as he saw me begin to walk up the beach, he turned away and melted into the crowd.

When I got there he had completely disappeared. It took me less than a minute to make my way up the slope and I was surprised that he could have disappeared so quickly.

After looking around in vain I saw Bert Cummings, who owns the fishing tackle shop in the High Street. He was standing with his hands in his pockets and his pipe clamped in his jaw, surveying the scene before him. His face was thunderous and I wondered why; but then knowing Bert I was sure I would soon find out.

'Hi! Bert! Where'd he go?' I called out.

Bert turned to me, slowly removing a hand from his trousers pocket to take the pipe out of his mouth.

'Good day, Mr Horribine. Who were you after?'

'Why, the tall man in the black coat, with the hat. He walked right past you.'

Bert gave me a long look before he said, only half to me, or so it seemed, 'Him? I wonder what you'd want with him, now?' And then, more directly, 'No, Mr Horribine, I didn't see him leave.'

I was surprised at that. I had watched him walk so close to Bert that he might have reached out and touched him, but I knew better than press the matter. Once again, Bert was gazing at me with that strange look, one of his eyebrows raised, as if he were confronted with something he could not quite make out. Then, suddenly, Bert stabbed into the air with his pipe-stem.

'Is that him over there?' he demanded. I followed the line of the pipe-stem with my eye, and sure enough, on the opposite side of the excavation, with his back to the sea, was the stranger. I have no idea how he got there so quickly.

'Yes, it is,' I said.

'D'you know him?'

'No, I just saw him watching and he seemed interesting. I thought I'd try to get a couple of lines for the paper, that's all.'

'Interesting? I'll say he's interesting. But I doubt he'd have anything to say to you, Mr Horribine.'

'Do you know him? I've not seen him around."

'No, Mr Horribine, I've never clapped my eyes on him before today.' His voice was measured, cautious; then his face cleared a little and he clamped the pipe back where he usually kept it.

'D'you mind telling me what they're planning to do now, Mr Horribine?' he asked.

'They're going to remove the stumps after the man from Historic Scotland has measured the site.'

Bert shook his head. 'I don't think that's a good idea at all,' he said slowly.

'Well, they can't just destroy them and they can't shift the sewer.'

'Sewer, to hell. The folk here have been doing their business in the sea for what? Eight hundred? A thousand? Two thousand? Maybe even more years? Eight hundred since the town got its charter, anyway, and there were people here long before that.'

'Oh, aye, Bert, but you know how it is; it's the modern world, and the new regulations say…'

'Aye, maybe, but they were written before they found that!' he exclaimed, with a passion in his voice that really took me aback. Again he stabbed into the air with the pipe, this time into the gaping pit below. I tried to break in, but Bert was in full song now, and anyone who knows Bert knows he would have his say.

'There are things in this world no man should meddle with. And that's one of them. You mark my words, Mr Horribine, there's something not right about all this, and the best thing to do would be to cover all that up *right now* and hope to hell it's not too late.'

Bert Cummings held some firm views on the subject of digging up that which had long been buried, and he gave full vent to them. At the time I was surprised; everyone in the town knew Bert and his opinions, but mostly they were about fishing, shooting and politics.


Had I known then what I know now, I would have agreed with Bert, but there was nothing either of us could have done about it. The site and those artefacts were either to be torn up and put in a museum, or torn up and thrown aside, because that sewer was going to go ahead.

The upshot was that I forgot about the man in the long coat. Bert was giving me all I needed in the way of a story, and I'm a newspaperman, not an amateur detective. A good row story was manna from heaven for me, and here I had one.

Once I had interviewed him and taken his picture against the backdrop of the site, I thought I'd get the other side of the story and went back down the slope.

David was busy taking pictures of the carvings on the stakes, which projected about four and a half feet above the sand. In between snaps he gave me plenty of information to counter Bert's view. In passing I also learned that he had no place to put up, although he did not see that as a problem. He reckoned he'd be up most of the night working anyway.

It was by that time, I suppose, about four in the afternoon. I was impressed by his dedication to duty; he was excited about the find, and kept saying, 'Yes, yes, of course – it's just perfect!'

I could see that he would work until he was ready to drop and then catch a few miserable hours sleep in his car, rather than waste time looking for a hotel, so I offered him a bed in our spare room. My children have both grown up and flown the nest, but they do like to visit, so we always had a couple of rooms ready.

He accepted gratefully, saying that if it was really no trouble then he'd be delighted. I suggested that he might bring his bags up to the house in the evening and have something to eat with us, and then he could come back and get on with his work. I would give him a key to the house and he could come and go as he pleased.


That is how your brother came to be staying with us at the time of his death, and also how it came about that I was to be responsible for settling his affairs. My wife and I both found David so easy to get along with that, when he decided to extend his stay for several weeks to go on studying the relics, we would hear nothing of his moving. His company was a delight, and he was a tidy golfer too; we shared many a pleasant three-ball when he was not working late into the night, in the clammy gloom of the old fish-market.

But to go back to the beach; the next day dawned sour and wet, a break in a long spell of fine weather. David had done well during the night and had finished measuring and drawing around three in the morning. He came up to the house to grab a little rest and a shower before getting back to the site for seven, when the contractor's men would be ready to work.

You would never have thought that this was a man who had scarce had three hours sleep, though; he was fizzing with energy and enthusiasm, always seeming to be in two places at once as he supervised the digger operators.

First, each of the perimeter stakes, which were about eight feet long and six inches square, were covered with sacking, and a rope was tied round them. Then, one by one, the ropes were hooked onto the arm of a digger and the stakes gently drawn out of the sand.

I remember thinking how delicately the machines handled the timbers – those drivers were skilled men. They were then quickly wrapped in sacking and polythene sheet before being laid on a trailer.

All the time David was scuttling to and fro, his mobile phone to one ear, while in the other hand he held a little walkie-talkie. A big crowd had come to see the show, despite the dirty weather.

I can't remember seeing the man with the hostile gaze at first; but when all the perimeter stakes had been removed and carted away, suddenly I caught sight of him.

The sun had come out again by then, and there he was, in that great black coat that fell almost to his feet and simply hung on him as if there was nothing but bones to hold it up. His back wasto the sun, his broad-brimmed hat casting a dark shadow over the steely, glittering eyes. I thought for a moment of going over to speak to him, but I was distracted by the next stage of the excavation.

The time was now just after eleven, and the moment had come for the most delicate part of the job; removing the huge stump at the centre of the circle. A digger clanked forward on its caterpillar tracks. The stump had already been covered with wet sacking for protection and a chain tied around it; this was then hooked onto the digger arm.

When all was ready I saw David give the signal to lift, his index finger aloft, making a rotating movement.  I heard the roar of the machine's engine deepen as the driver took the strain. But there was no movement from the stump. The engine got louder and louder, and the tracks at the front began to sink into the sand, until the driver backed off his throttle, let his machine idle, and came down from his cab, scratching his head.

There followed a brief conference before a team of men were summoned to dig away and loosen the sand around the tree with shovels.

After about an hour of this the roots of the tree had been cleared to a depth of three feet or so. The digger driver looked, nodded, got back into his cab, and applied the strain again. Great black belches of diesel smoke poured from the digger's exhaust and the roar of engine drowned out all other noise.

At first, as before, nothing happened. Then the bellow of the machine deepened and it began to cant forward on its tracks again. I could see the determined look on the driver's face.

Slowly the stump began to move, at first almost imperceptibly. Then suddenly it leapt up as if it had been blown out of the sand by an explosion, throwing the digger back on its tracks in clattering recoil. Several large stones were hurled into the air by the violence of the movement and one smashed against the cab with a ferocious bang.

Instinctively I ducked and I heard a shout from the crowd. Turning, I saw that one of the contractor's men had fallen to his knees on the sand, obviously injured. His gloved hands were pressed to his face and blood was streaming between his fingers.

I don't know why, but as others rushed to help him, I remember looking to see what the tall man's reaction was; perhaps I had already had some inkling of his malevolent nature. But he had gone.

The injured man had been hit in the face by a sharp stone which had cut his cheek. At least this was what we reckoned must have happened. He could not remember a thing about it, except that something had whizzed past his face at the moment the stump had been dragged from the sand.

I think we all believed that he was lucky that it had not been a larger stone, else it would have taken his head off. But the man had been standing well back from the stump when the accident had happened. Everyone was surprised that a stone could have flown so far. The cut stopped bleeding within a few minutes, but nevertheless he was sent up to the hospital to have it dressed.

Naturally all of this kept me busy and I did not notice the stump being loaded onto the trailer and carted away.

Once all the stakes and the central stump had been taken to the old fish-market, the interest of both media and local people waned. The work on the beach continued and life went back to normal.

David had the artefacts arranged on the floor of the building as they had been on the beach, and began to study them in greater detail.

I sometimes went up to see him at work, though to tell the truth I didn't like it much. It was cold and clammy in there, what with all the wet sacking, but worse, there was the most infernal stink. Even with the doors wide open, a ghastly smell of decay and corruption filled the place.

We had, as I explained, invited your brother to stay with us, and our lives settled into a routine. From Monday to Friday, David would work, sometimes late into the night, measuring and drawing, and then come up to the house for a late supper before bed; and on the weekends we would golf or go for walks.

During these excursions he explained to me what was so exciting to him about the discovery. The structure was covered in runic writing, which had been used by the Vikings. It had been, according to the prevailing view, developed from Roman lettering, modified to make it easy for carving.

He said he was sure that the structure was from about the third century. This would make it early for a Viking one, possibly the earliest in the country. Everything hinged on deciphering the runes and finding out what was written there. David was convinced that this was an important find.

To save time here, I think you should read the diary for the 17th of August till the 21st.

*(Excerpt)*

*17/8* I have just got back to the H's house after a long day working on the inscription on the perimeter posts. I think I made a break-through today. Each of the posts has a column of runes on it, which I had thought spelled out words. But I could not get them to work in any Scandinavian language that I know of.

Tonight I tried something else, to see if the writing went along – that is, reading each post in turn. I found that I could make a name, reading right to left, on the first six posts – 'Gunnar', which is a common Norse name. So it looks as if the inscription runs *around* the entire structure, and not up and down each individual post as I thought.

*18/8* I began to transcribe the top line of the runes. It takes a long time to do but I am sure that my theory is right. I have managed to make, translated into English, 'I Gunnar of Helmsvik'.

This is fascinating. Gunnar of Helmsvik is the hero of a little known saga. His son was taken and killed by the followers of Loki, the evil brother of Odin. Gunnar swore to hunt down and destroy all those who worshipped Loki. If this site is really directly related to him, then it is a major find.

*19/8* I worked late tonight – later than I had planned to. It's hard work, transcribing the runes, as I have to unwrap each post in turn and copy the runes onto a piece of paper, then wrap the wood up again to protect it.

The smell was really bad tonight. It seems to be coming from the central stump. The posts don't seem to be so bad. Maybe there is a fish or something rotting in there.

*20/8* I am getting on well with copying the runes now. It's a pity to have wasted so much time trying to make sense of them reading up and down the posts, but I think I can finish by the middle of next week. I saw old Raincoat again, standing on the other side of the harbour. How he survives in that get-up in this heat is beyond me.

*21/8* Another good day, so I should be cheery, but a feeling of depression is beginning to creep up on me. I think it must be that hellish stink – it's even worse now, or seems so. It's as if there were a dead body in there.

And there's something else – I've been feeling it for a while now – as if someone was watching all the time. Sometimes I think I see something moving-out of the corner of my eye – something dark. It's like a dark shadow – a globe of pure blackness, with tentacles. I know that sounds crazy, but I've seen it – or I believe I have seen it – several times. When I turn round there's nothing there, of course. Still it's creepy. I think I might be getting over-tired – copying out these runes is so time-consuming – they're hard to make out. I'm going to stick to my routine and take the weekend off, even though I'm keen to get the inscription down and translated.

It was hot and sunny again today, and guess who was on the other side of the harbour? Anyway, had a good lunch at the pub with RH – playing golf tomorrow, then he promises to take me along the cliff path with Mrs H and the dogs, which should be fine – at least the sea breeze will be cool and fresh.

*(End of extract)*

I am sure that you will agree that your brother, while progressing well with the work he had set himself, was disturbed by certain unusual phenomena.

At the time I had no knowledge of this; David always put on his best face with us and certainly never discussed any shadows that he thought he had seen. Not then, anyway. And for my part, since that moment on the beach when the black stump was torn from its lair, I had never again seen the ominous figure of that dark stranger. But obviously David had, regularly; and I have seen him again, more recently.

At that time we were busy at the Chronicle. It was the beginning of the school year, so there was the usual round of new intakes to be photographed. Since I shared the photographic duties as well as editing the paper and writing the leaders, I had plenty to fill my time.

Another story had broken that had my deputy scratching his head; it appeared that Seaforth had, for want of a better word, a cat-napper. A number of people who lived at the harbour end of town had reported to the police that their beloved pets had gone missing. Checks by police officers turned nothing up. It was a good story, but no-one seemed to be able to get anywhere with it, even when the number of missing cats went into double figures.

Hindsight is a funny thing; but at that time I made no connection between the discovery on the beach and the missing cats, a connection that now seems so obvious.

Then something happened that made me think strange thoughts in the wee small hours when I lay awake.

One day I bumped into Bert Cummings. He was in the Harbour Bar when I dropped in for an after-work pint; he stood at the bar, a pint jar before him, his pipe jammed in his jaws. I went to speak to him, because Bert was always good for a yarn or two and quite a few of these had already made it into my Local Knowledge page.

It was unusual to find Bert in that pub – it was off his beaten track – so I asked him, once we'd exchanged greetings, how he came to be there.

He said, after a moment's hesitation, and one of those crooked glances, 'I came down after that great long streak in black we saw on the beach; mind, you were after him yourself.'

This was the first I had heard of the dark stranger since then and I was taken aback; he was such a distinctive character that he could hardly have hidden himself. Yet it appeared that he was still in the town, if Bert were to be believed; and Bert Cummings didn't miss much.

'I haven't seen him – you mean he's still here?'

'Och, aye, Mr Horribine, he's still here all right; I've seen him hanging about a few times. I don't like the air about him, and I made up my mind to ask what his business was. I'm not a prying sort of a lad usually, but I've had enough of his creeping and sneaking – him and that black dog of his. Not that I've ever seen a dog like that before.'

'Did you catch up with him?'

'No. He came down to the harbour and by the time I turned the corner he'd disappeared; just vanished, like. I tell you, he can't half shift when he's a mind to. But when he's still it's as if he was a shadow painted on the wall. But whenever he sees me coming he's off.'

'It's funny; I don't remember him having a dog down on the beach.'

'Aye, I know. I never saw it myself till that digger pulled up the stump, but it must have been there all the time, scuffling about in the sand. As soon as that stump was lifted, your man gave a shout and the dog ran over. Near bowled that guy that cut his face clean over – I supposed it had gotten a fright or something with all the noise.

'The next thing, it's away with your man, jumping up and down at his side like a puppy that hadn't seen its master for a week – some puppy, though! Black as night and a great shaggy beast. There was another thing – his coat was all wet, like as if he'd been in the sea. And here's something else too – maybe I shouldn't be telling you this, but I'm not just entirely sure that dog didn't jump out from under that hellish stump.'

An awkward silence followed this last and then Bert looked at me, this time troubling to take the pipe out of his mouth. He spoke in a low voice, gruff with urgency, his eyes flashing.

'Likely you'll think I'm just a daft old blether, Mr Horribine, being as how you've lived in London and all; but I'll tell you something you don't know. My mother had the sight and so did her mother before her; and I have it too – not all the time, but just now adn again I get to see things other folk – well, let's just say I get to see the other side.

'Not many people know that, for I've no desire to have every damn gowk in town at my shop annoying me to read their tea-leaves or do the pools for them or get a hold of Auntie Iris that's been dead twenty years or whatever, but I know you'll not let on.

'Mr Horribine, I'd say that was no ordinary mortal man, and that hellish beast was not whelped of any bitch that lives in this world; and I'm as sure as I'm standing here afore you that no good'll come from it walking in the same world where common mortal folk like you and me walk.'

I was at a loss for something to say, but at the same time the hackles on the back of my neck rose, for Bert had struck a nerve with that. Instinctively, I looked out the window; the evening sun was sinking over the row of houses that front the harbour, casting long deep shadows over the quay; the end to a perfect day.

'Is that why you were so against the relics on the beach being touched?'

'Aye,' said Bert, 'It was that. I knew there was something there – something that hadn't been touched or seen the light of day for more years than a body could dream; something that had whimpered and whined in its loneliness all those terrible long years, something bitter, black and unclean that just waited till it could get itself free; something that somebody put there, meaning that it should never, ever be free again; and bound it there with a cursed spell that wound round and round those black posts like a line on a reel; a cursed spell that warned anybody with the brains to read it never to tamper nor interfere with what lay there; a spell that was broken when the stump was lifted.'

Bert stopped, looked away and drained his pint. 'I must be getting along, Mr Horribine,' he said. 'You'll maybe think I've said enough, but some things have to be said. But before I go, I'll tell you something else. See, any sight I've had before this has been safe enough; you might say like watching a picture show, except all around. I've seen this town as it was eight hundred years ago, when we got the Charter, seen it as clear as you see the High Street today.

I've seen Viking raiders on the Low Common, the weird glow of distant burning houses lighting their eyes, drunk as lords and staggering under the weight of their loot.

'But I knew it was all just shadows and not real, like footprints in the sand the next tide would wash away, as if somewhere a window had been opened that let me see through to the other side.

'But – and you mark my words, Mr Horribine – my mother, now she had the sight much stronger than me. She saw things she'd far rather not, things that were as real as you and me standing here, that frightened the poor woman near out of her wits. She would never set foot down at that end of the beach even in broad daylight. But nothing like that ever happened to me till now.

'Well, let me tell you, as far as I'm concerned, that fellow and his dog count as something *I'd* rather not have seen, and I've an idea I know now what it was that kept my mother away from there. It took me some guts to follow that character down here, striding along the High Street in his black coat with his great big dog and nobody else knowing that he was there at all. I'm glad he never turned to look at me and maybe I'm relieved to not have caught up with them, if I'm honest.

'That pair's hanging about here for to do mischief, and – and, well, Mr Horribine, I know the lad's staying with you and Mrs H, so I'm duty bound to tell you; I think they mean your archaeologist no good at all. I think they know it was him had the spell broken, and I would get him away back to Edinburgh as quick as you can – and out from under your roof.'

He turned to leave. 'Mr Horribine?' he asked as he pulled open the door. 'Did he look at you? That day on the beach?'

I nodded. 'He stared at me with the most menacing gaze I think I have ever seen,' I replied, slowly.

'I don't like the sound of that, Mr Horribine. I would lock my doors at night.'


A few days later, I met the Clerk of Works after a local councillor's surgery.

We chatted after the meeting had closed. I wanted to clarify a couple of points for my story. When I had done, I asked – trying hard not to appear as if I were posing a leading question – how things went with the workman who had been injured. The Clerk frowned deeply.

'Oh yes. He recovered from the cut – it was nothing. He was back at work two days later. But last week he was taken ill again, and things have gone badly; he's in intensive care, I'm afraid. It seems he has some strange form of pneumonia.'

He looked at me significantly. 'I don't think you can connect the two – I mean the accident and the illness…'

'Of course not,' I said, to reassure him. As we were about to leave, I turned to him again.

'Listen – that day on the beach – I don't suppose you noticed a tall chap, dressed all in black?

The Clerk frowned again. 'No, I can't say I did. Mind, there was a lot going on. What was he doing?'

'Oh nothing; he just stood and watched, a little apart from the crowd. It was just that he was a stranger and I wondered if you knew him. Might have had a dog with him, a black dog?'

The Clerk of Works again shook his head thoughtfully, and then he snapped his pale blue eyes up to meet mine. 'Wait a minute,' he said, his voice surprised. 'Did you say a black dog?'

'Yes, a big one. Might have been rooting around near the stump.'

'Really? Well, I never saw any man in black nor a black dog; but I did speak to the site foreman yesterday about the man who was injured – the one in hospital.'

'Yes?' I interjected.

'Well, he said that he'd been up to visit the poor lad the night before. They would only let him in for a few minutes. Said the man was half delirious – probably from the medication – and he was plugged into all sorts of machines. But he apparently – listen, this is off the record, isn't it?' The Clerk of Works paused, searching my face with a worried look. 'Only, you know, I wouldn't want to be quoted –'

'Yes, of course,' I reassured him. 'I'm just curious, that's all. It's not a story.'

'Well then, Roger, I know it's just the ravings of a sick man, but Sandy said that the poor lad kept asking him if he'd seen a black dog. Sandy said he seemed to be absolutely terrified of this black dog, and convinced it was after him. Nothing Sandy could say would placate him, and eventually he had to call for the nurse.'

I wish to impress upon you that fantastic as they may seem, the phenomena I describe were seen and felt by others. At that time I had not, other than on the beach, seen the tall man in black, and I had never seen the black dog.

Mind, I *did* see something fly out of the hole and strike the workman when the stump was ripped up. It hadn't looked much like a stone to me; but then it hadn't looked much like a dog, either. More like a deep black shadow, small and intense, with – maybe – tentacles or long legs. But until the night I met Bert I had really forgotten all about it.

David came home late that night so I did not have a chance to talk to him, though I had made up my mind that I should, and quickly.

It was not that I really believed that some supernatural influence had been let loose – not then anyway. In fact I had half a mind that the poor man in the hospital was suffering from extreme delusions as a result of his illness. At that time, of course, I had not seen David's diary; nor could I have foreseen the turn that events were about to take.

The next day I went down to the fish-market building at around eleven-thirty, ostensibly with the aim of offering to buy David a pub lunch, something we did regularly anyway. I was curious to see how he was doing. I had not been to see him at work for over a week, partly because I had been busy, but mostly because of the stink, which was enough to make you retch when you walked in.

When I got down there and slid open door, the smell hit me like a physical blow. I stood on the threshold, hanging onto the door-jamb, willing my limbs to take me into the clammy interior. David looked up as I entered. He was wearing a surgeon's face-mask.

'Come in, come in,' he said, springing to his feet. 'Or shall I come out? It's a bit whiffy in here today.'

'You can say that again,' I wheezed. 'But I'll come in. I'd like to see what's doing. I've never smelt anything like it. Is this normal in your line of work?'

'No it's not. To tell you the truth it's got me worried,' came the reply. 'I've taken every precaution to protect the relics, but even so I think they must be undergoing some sort of accelerated decay. The stump is the worst, but the posts have been affected too. Their surfaces are breaking up rapidly and I'm afraid that if I don't get them into some sort of permanent storage facility soon I may lose them entirely.'

'Good grief,' I said. 'That would be a tragedy.'

'It would indeed. I've already talked to my boss about it and we plan to ship the artefacts to Leith tomorrow, where we can get them into a cold storage unit.'

We were now in the centre of the shed, having slowly walked across the floor as we talked. The stump – from which the worst of the stink seemed to be emanating – was I suppose about four or five feet away. It was a massive timber, fully four feet in diameter and about twelve feet long.

The trunk section had been supported on trestles in order to prevent damage to the roots, which formed a ball at the end of the log and were still largely intact. It was shrouded in brown jute sackcloth, which in turn was wrapped up in polythene sheeting. On the floor by it was a hose-pipe which, David explained, allowed him to douse everything with sea water regularly.

We were standing – I now had a handkerchief to my face – looking at the stump, when I suddenly thought I saw something with the corner of my eye. It was a dense black shadow that seemed to whip across the floor from the roots of the stump and then back again. I turned, but saw nothing. David, however, noticed my movement.

*'Did you see it?'* he hissed.

'I thought I saw – I thought I saw a black shadow come out from the roots and make towards you. But when I turned to look it had vanished. It must just be an effect of coming in from the bright sun.'

'My God. Did you really see it? You did, didn't you? Oh, Jesus.' And with that poor David slumped to a squat and ran his hand through his thinning hair. 'I don't know whether to be happy or sad; happy because I'm not going mad, after all, or sad because – because if you've seen it too then I can't deny its existence any longer.'

'What do you mean?'

'Oh, Roger,' he said, rising to his feet wearily. 'Let's not beat about the bush. You saw him on the beach that day too.'

Of course I knew whom he was referring to, and he was right; the time for prevarication was long past. So I told him about the conversations I'd had with Bert Cummings. Naturally he shook his head in sceptical disbelief; after all, he was a man of science. But he paled when he heard about the man in the intensive care unit and his terror of a black dog.

He waited till I had finished before he spoke. 'I've seen that dog; and I've heard him. I hear him growling and snuffling outside the doors at night. At first I thought it was just a local mutt attracted by the smell – but the fact is that no ordinary dog will come near the place. I've watched them – they just won't come within fifty yards of the shed; then they yelp and run, their tails between their legs. You won't see any dogs or cats near the harbour now. And there's another thing: listen.'

I listened, and then said I couldn't hear anything at all.

'I know,' he said grimly. 'It takes a minute or so to cotton on, but I'll make it easy. This is a commercial harbour, Roger; shouldn't there be seagulls?'

'But of course there are seagulls,' I protested. But then my heart froze. He was right. All I could hear was the distant rumble of traffic in the town. No seagulls. In a town which is legendary for the seagull population. None at all. Not one. Total and complete silence.

'It's been like that since I brought these things here,' David continued, his face pale. 'I've been denying everything to myself, but it's all true. You know I have just deciphered the last part of the runic inscription? What a triumph; no one has ever discovered such a lengthy inscription in runes before.' He shook his head. 'But at what cost? At what cost?'

'David, what do you mean?' I was looking at him earnestly – I am taller than he was, and he was between me and the tree-stump, so as I looked I had a clear view of the stump behind him. 'Are you saying that you – *good God!*'

'What?' exclaimed David, whirling round. 'What did you –'

But there was no need for him to continue. I could see by the sag of his shoulders that he had also seen. Impossible though it might have been, the jute sacking over the roots of the tree-stump was *moving* – not just moving, either, but squirming, as if some nameless tentacled horror was wriggling beneath it.

I must admit I was for running there and then, but David was too much of a scientist for that. Covering his face again, and donning his safety glasses and rubber gloves, he approached the heaving bundle with a resolute stride.

He kneeled down beside the stump and began to peel back the layers of polythene and sacking; when he got to the last layer I could see his hand shaking. Then he flicked away the jute sacking and the greatest horror I have ever seen confronted my terrified eyes.

First, the miasma of decay and corruption that instantly flooded the shed was so intense – a hundred times worse than before – that we both choked and coughed. Then, almost in the same instant, a great swarm of hellish black flies – huge, foul insects – flew out and buzzed about us, crawling on our hands, faces and clothes till they were quite black with a squirming second skin. And then we saw the worst; from inside the rootball of the tree, in states of putrefaction more sickening than anything I had ever seen, fell the mangled corpses of at least a dozen cats.

David turned his head – he was still kneeling by the tree. '*Get out!*' he yelled. 'Save yourself!'

As he said these words he was thrown back by a foul blast as a dense black shadow whizzed out of the root-ball and struck him on the face, knocking him down.

I ran forward, fighting through the clouds – literally – of obscene flies, which now were settling all over his slumped body. I dragged him to his feet and, as I turned to the door, I saw, framed in it, the dread apparition of that tall gaunt man, his face in shadow, a huge black dog at his side. He seemed to be laughing.

Of course, when we got to the door there was no sign of either the man or his dog. But I noted, in the photographic way that you do when real terror is upon you, that in the doorway were the prints of wet feet – four paw-prints of a massive dog, and two bony out-lines where impossibly fleshless but unquestionably human feet had stood, but a moment before.

I am sorry to say that David was badly injured; he suffered weird lacerations to his face, which needed to be stitched. I called for an ambulance and accompanied him up to the hospital. Then I took him home, where my wife – who was naturally distraught – propped him into  bed and made him promise not to get up.

I dosed myself with a strong belt of the Morangie, and then phoned David's office to speak to his superior. I told him about the accident and that someone would have to come up immediately to take over the work. There would be no problem and David's chief promised to get to Seaforth that day.

I went back to see David, and told him what had happened. He smiled, and then said, 'James (who was his manager) will want all my notes; and of course he must have them. But I always make a copy and annotate it in my diary, which is here, in my bedside cabinet. Please don't give him that.'

Naturally I promised not to, if that was his wish. Then he went on; 'If something – if something should happen to me, I want you to read my diary.'

I protested – why should anything happen to him? – and so on – but he insisted. He made me promise to read and to make a copy of his journal. I already knew that he was not married and had no children of his own; but I did not know till then about you. He could only tell me that you now lived in the east of France. But he nevertheless insisted – despite my continued protestations – that I should find you and send you the diary, and tell you to read it. He was apologetic about all of this.

The rest of the story may be told briefly. James arrived later that afternoon and we immediately went to see the relics. He wanted to see David, but I told him that he was resting.

When we got to the old fish-market the first thing that I noted was that there was no overpowering stench – just a rather stale odour of seawater and sacking. Of cats – and I can tell you I had to steel my nerves to look – there was nothing at all; and perhaps there were a few flies circulating high in the roof. Outside in the sunshine I could hear the mewling of seagulls.

James was a pleasant man, older than David, and placid in temperament. He was a little disappointed in the state of the relics, saying that they had perished a good deal, but that they still could be preserved.

He was impressed with the work David had toiled so long over and he nodded approvingly when he saw the whole inscription copied out in his neat hand. But he was unable to read it; no, he said, David was the man for Scandinavian languages, he'd have to take this to the university for translation.

I saw him installed in the Benady Hotel and then went back to see David. He seemed much better and had slept. I allowed myself to believe that perhaps the whole thing was a hallucination, that David was over-tired. It was a case of wishful thinking, I am afraid.


At about two a.m. the next morning I was awakened by the sound of a dog howling – though it sounded more like a wolf. I sat up in bed, fumbling for the light. Then I heard a dreadful shriek, the like of which I hope never to hear again, coming from David's room. I burst open the door, flicking on the lights as I did so.

It seemed – well, it seemed to me that in the tails of my eyes several dark shadows, like balls of intense blackness, with tentacles, scurried into the corners, but when I looked I could see nothing.

David was dead. The whole bed was drenched and, later, at the inquest, it was revealed that his lungs had been full of fluid; a verdict was returned that he died as a result of a freakish and vicious form of infectious pneumonia.

I think that you should now read the last extract that I have marked in David's diary. It will explain his concern for you and yours. For myself I can only say that my wife and I have moved house twice since leaving Seaforth and are now resident in a small town far from the sea, living out of suitcases under false names.

Still, it may be too late for us by the time you get this letter; for I have already seen the man in the black coat and his dog, and the quickly moving shadows have found us again. I fear for us all now; something terrible has been done and I can see no way to undo it. God bless you and good luck.


Yours Sincerely,


*Roger Horribine.*


PS I am sure that the man in the black coat and his dog can only be seen in direct sunlight, and I think that their powers are weakest then; beware the shadows.


*(Extract)*


1/9: I have at last identified and copied down all of the runes. This is exciting; no message like this has been discovered before. The runes read:


*I Gunnar of Helmsvik have bound under the tree, by the magic taught to me by the witch Gretel, the great wolf Fenris, offspring and favour-ite of Loki, that no longer shall he scourge the earth with his wick-edness. We fought a great battle here with the followers of Loki and we have killed them all. Nine of my men, good and loyal to me, were slain in this battle, and I have bound their spirits here as Watchers. Round them I have set the wall upon which I have made this doom:*

*by these words know that he who raises the spell that binds the great wolf shall be bound to the great wolf himself and followed by him; and the great wolf shall lead the Watchers to him and he shall feel their bite, him and his family and all who aid him and all of theirs. I Gunnar of Helmsvik lay this curse to the end of days.*


*(End of extract)*


Jean Geddes' body was found when her housekeeper, as she had done every morning for the last twenty-three years, brought coffee and *pain au chocolat* to her bed-chamber. Madame had been well the evening before, the terrified servant confirmed, only too aware where the suspicion of the police might lead them. She herself had spent the evening at home with her family, who would vouch for her.

The preliminary opinion of the police was that Madame Geddes had been drowned by a person or persons unknown. The bed, the covers and the carpet in the bedroom in which she had been found were all drenched with water, and the dead woman's lungs were full of it.

To complicate matters, the pathologist said that had he not known for a fact that the woman had been fit and well the day before her death, he would have been happy to swear that she had been under water for a week. And to cap it all, it was sea-water. He had even found pieces of fresh seaweed in the dead woman's mouth and throat.


But Bligny-sur-Ouche, where the late Jean Geddes had lived and died, alone, *is over three hundred miles from the sea.*

*Historically-aware readers may have noticed the uncanny resemblance that the location of this story has with Holme Henge, otherwise known as 'Seahenge' discovered in 1998 at Holme Beach in Norfolk. I remember, from the reports that the time, a vociferous protestor who claimed that all sorts of terrible things would happen if the henge were to be removed. This formed the central part of the story.*

*Holme Henge is actually far older than the one in this story, but its builders had not, in 2049BCE, learned how to write, in order to leave a curse for its discoverers! So I was obliged to change its dates a little.*

*The old fish-market, to which the timbers were taken, is still there, at Arbroath harbour, where the story is set.*

# Scene Through a Window

I had been on holiday in France, when I was suddenly called back because of an illness – a very severe one – in the family. It happened that the nearest airport from which I could get a flight home was Lyon, so I made my reservation and got myself there as soon as I possibly could.

Unfortunately it was high summer and the traditional season for the French air traffic controllers to hold the government – and the passengers – to ransom, and I of course, landed unlucky. My flight was delayed for a period 'not yet determined'. Lyon, it seemed, was not to receive even the quota of flights that it merited *pro rata*, with all resources being diverted to Paris.

The airline staff offered us blanket ands sandwiches in the departure lounge. We would leave on the first available flight out, connecting to our destinations outside French airspace.

Most of us settled down quickly, it being quite late by that time, after 11 o'clock at night. A few night-owls like me sat together and chatted, filling ourselves up with coffee and sandwiches. I have to admit, I had a few liveners to chase away the gloom.

Amongst our number was one, tall, with greying hair, well covered – quite unexceptional, except that he constantly looked around himself rather nervously, and he was wearing a cravat. A cravat is an unusual piece of attire these days, especially when not accompanied by sports jacket and slacks. The man had the habit of fretting with it as if he was not used to wearing one.

It could have been because of an unseasonable throat infection, but my profession alerts me to these details. I noted them, thinking that a tale thereby must hang, if only it could be prised out.


Fairly soon the group had shrunk to four or five of us lounging around on rather hard sofas which we had arranged into a square. There was myself, the odd cravat wearer, a young man from Bristol, and a middle aged couple from Glasgow. The female part of this was snuggled tight into the shoulder of her partner under a coat.

She took little part in the proceedings except to smile and nod from time to time and sip from a large mug of coffee which she had liberally laced with brandy. Wise girl, I thought.

One by one we outlined our reasons for being there. I told of my worries, to muted clucks of sympathy, the young man from Bristol explained that he had been sent on a business trip by a new employer and was needed back urgently, the couple from Glasgow were to attend a big family wedding on the weekend and did not want to be late.

'So what about you, then,' I asked of the cravat wearer, whose name, prosaically enough, was Jim Willis. He seemed friendly enough, and it was clear that he preferred company to being alone, so I thought the boldness of my approach was reasonable. I could hardly have foreseen his reaction. Involuntarily he clutched at his throat and then looked quickly around.

'Oh, it's all right,' I quickly interposed. 'I didn't mean to put you on the spot.' Which of course I had, really.

However, Jim just stared into the distance for a moment and then dropped his head into his hands, his shoulders heaving with a deep shuddering sigh that ran through the whole of his body. The rest of us looked at each other uncomfortably, and for a moment I felt very embarrassed, but then he looked up.

'No,' he said, as if answering a question, 'You're quite right. I should tell you my story – even though not a one of you here will believe it.'

Again the rest of us shot glances at each other, but this time of quickening interest. Inwardly I felt vindicated – my hunch had been correct, here was a tale at last.


Jim began slowly, uncertainly.

'I bought a house in Burgundy last year, you see.' He paused, and gathered himself.

'Yes,' he went on, this time in a firmer voice. 'I bought a house in Burgundy last year and now I am going to sell it – if I can. I have always loved France, and that area in particular. I am an architect by profession, and tinkering with old houses is my hobby too.

My wife and I had decided to retire to rural France. We spent ages looking for a place, over years of visits, and had a lot of fun too; but everything we saw was either too small, too big, too run down, too modern. We had an image in our mind's eye of what we wanted, and we just could not find it. Indeed, it had got to the point where we were ready to give up on Burgundy and look further south when we found it.

'We had been in the office of an estate agent – a fat old rogue who had once been a lawyer. This particular agent had shown us quite a few properties. Unfortunately he had a distinct idea of what it was that we wanted, which was not the same as ours. We were sitting opposite him at his desk as he was hurriedly going through particulars with a frown on his face when he passed over one that caught my eye – a traditional Burgundy house with a little watchtower – what they call an *échaugette* there. I immediately asked why he hadn't shown us that one.

'The agent's frown deepened. Oh no, that one was not for us. It was too far away, it was too big, it was this, it was that. But I persisted and so did my wife. She reached over and pulled the file out of the bundle, to our man's obvious displeasure, though of course he was much too polite to say anything.

Anyway, after some mumbling and grumbling, he said that he did have another property in *that* village on his books, one that might actually be right for us. We could look at that and by the way have a look at this other that so interested us. So we drove up.

'You couldn't miss the house with the *échaugette*. It was right in the middle of the village, overlooking the square, on top of a hill, opposite the church. My wife and I looked at each other and we both knew at once that that was the one for us. But still we had to go and look at this other house that the agent proposed – another badly 'renovated' wreck full of the ugliest modern finishings. All completely out of keeping with the building, which was nothing special anyway, and grossly overpriced.

'We retrieved the key to "our" house from the cafe where it was normally kept and pried into its gloomy depths.

'What a revelation it was! Under the years of filth and grime and cobwebs was a real medieval French town house – yes it had been mucked about, but there was enough left to make it possible to restore it. And the price – even the price the fat old rogue was *asking* was cheap.

'To cut a long story short, the next day we made an offer and the week after that we signed the preliminary papers. The agent clearly thought that we were quite mad to want it, but his relief at finding a buyer was clearly too much for him to risk the sale by protesting.'

Here Jim paused in his narrative, and sipped reflectively from his glass. When he took up the tale again, his voice had changed.

'All last winter we had work done on the place. All the rubbish – lorryloads of it – that the previous owner had accumulated, was loaded up and tipped. The upper apartment on the first floor, which was more-or-less liveable, we had cleaned and redecorated, and a new bathroom suite put into – of all places – the little watchtower. It amused us to have it there and it seemed a practical move – there was already a convenience and a cold water supply there.

'While these basic works were being done, I flew over when I could and checked on the progress. By early this summer it looked as if the place was ready to live in. So my wife and I drove over with the kids to spend a month happily pottering in our new project – or so we thought.'

Jim stopped again here, and the weight of some gravely troubling memory seemed to press down on his shoulders. At length he began his narrative again.

'Well, I was all gung-ho for some practical work. I wanted to tackle some rendering on the *échaugette*, which was badly needing help. So on the first day I got out the ladder and my pointing hammer and wire brush and got on with the task of preparing the brickwork for a coat of lime render.'

Jim looked up and laughed, the first time he had done so during his story. 'You may not realise that an architect spends most of his time organising projects from an office, attending meetings and pampering clients. Actually working on buildings is a rare pleasure indeed.

'Anyway, I had been chipping and brushing away in the sun, thoroughly enjoying myself and looking forward to the cheese and good local wine we had bought in for lunch, when I tapped a loose flake of the old render and a piece about a foot square fell right off.

'That was surprising enough – it had looked quite sound to me. But even more so was the fact that under the flake of mortar there was a little window – about six by four inches. Quite clearly, someone had rendered over it deliberately. More to the point, someone – probably the same person – had plastered up the window on the *inside* as well.

'Now the *échaugette* was pretty dim. So maybe the fact that someone had gone to the lengths that they had to block up the tiny peephole should have made me think a moment, I'll grant you. But I didn't. I was so thrilled to find this original feature that I rushed to tell my wife, who was just as pleased.

'The rest of the day I spent clearing the plaster from both sides of the window, so that by the late afternoon and time for aperitifs the job was finished.

'The house is on a crossroads, and it was built when the bandits in the area were not just retired lawyers but lawless thugs who preyed upon the villagers. The *échaugette* served a real purpose, a defensive one, and it had, as was now revealed, three – rather than two – windows, all about the same size, large enough to fire a crossbow or a pistol through, but small enough to protect whoever was inside from return fire.

'From these three windows the two walls of the house could be covered in security. In addition they each a gave a clear sight-line down one of the three roads that crossed outside.

'The one I had discovered looked onto the square in front of the bouse. It also gave a clear view of anyone who might knock at the front door.'

'I was thoroughly pleased with this day's work. The next day I patted myself on the back again for a job well done, and moved onto other tasks.'


Jim paused and the plump Glaswegian woman smiled at him. 'Go on,' she said. 'You're just getting to the best bit, aren't you?'

Jim laughed a nervous, mirthless laugh. 'I'm sorry about all these details, but they're important – you see, I now know that the window was blocked up for a reason, and not just so that the previous owner could fix a toilet cabinet to the inside of it.'

''Really?' I inquired, my ears pricking up at this.

He nodded. 'A week or so later another couple came out from England to visit us and we had a fine weekend with them. We visited a few local *caves* to stock up on wine, went down to Beaune for the market, had lunch in a café, It was a really nice Burgundy day out, under that glorious blue sky and brilliant sunshine, then back up to our house to spend the next few days in the warmth of the courtyard.

'We had dinner outside, *coq au vin*, the *coq* being supplied by a neighbour, followed by excellent cheese, wine and chat till long after the bats began to flit through the air above our heads and the stars began to twinkle.

'That was two weeks ago. It was the first night that we had really enjoyed our new home-from-home, the first night that it had lived up to expectations; and unfortunately the last, too.

'The night after our friends left, I slept fitfully. It was hot and the air seemed oppressive and heavy. Our house is in the hills and I could feel a change coming on. There was thunder in the air.

'I suppose about three in the morning it broke, with a dreadful clattering of thunder that echoed around the hills for an age and a blinding flash of lightning.

'Instinctively I got up to check that the windows and shutters were all closed, because already blasts of wind were whipping around the house. When I had done, I looked in on the children, who were soundly asleep as though nothing was happening. Then I went to the *échaugette* to fetch a drink of water from the tap there.

'You have no idea how I wish I had not, now. I poured the glass – the water in our village is really delicious, you know, they ought to bottle it – and drained it. As I did so there came another crackling boom of thunder and a brilliant flash, even closer than before, that lit up the whole of the scene before me – through the little peep-hole I was so proud to have uncovered.'

At this his hand rose once again to his throat and stayed there. At length, and it seemed with great difficulty, he continued, his voice now shaking.

'You can't imagine what I saw in that flash of lightning. A band of men – armed men – were crowded around the front door of the house! I couldn't help but look more closely, obviously. It was quite dark outside because the village streetlamps are switched off in the wee hours, but somehow or another the scene seemed to have its own illumination. So I could quite clearly see what was going on.

'As I pressed closer to the peep-hole I could see that this light, this hellish, orange light, came from a building on fire further away on the other side of the square. I thought at first it was the Town House but I quickly realised that it wasn't. I had no idea what building it was – because I had never seen it before, not in all my exploration of the village.

'By this same glow I could see that here and there, lying on the ground, were shapes that at first looked like bundles of rags that had been cast aside. Then I realised, to my complete horror, that they were bodies – bodies with dark blood all round them.

'The men in front of the house were wearing strange clothes: rusty cuirasses, helmets, bucklers and long boots. They carried spears and axes and battle-notched swords.

'I realised that by some agency outside of myself I was peering into a vision from some time long in the past. I thought that I must have been dreaming – but what a dream! So vivid, so exact. The men were shouting in angry, drunken voices in a dialect I had never heard before but which by some strange means I could understand. They were calling for someone by name – to come out. And though it was not my name that they called, I knew that it was nevertheless me whom they wished to parley with.

'I don't know why, but I wasn't frightened, not then. I didn't understand what I was seeing, but still it seemed far enough away. It was creepy rather than frightening.

'Then I got a real shock. I turned to leave the *échaugette* and opened the door into the bedroom. Where my wife should have been sleeping soundly in the darkness, there was candlelight and an open fire, and a woman I had never seen before gazing at me with terrified eyes, huddling two sobbing children to her.

'I say I had never seen the woman before, and I had not, yet I knew she was my wife, and that those were my children. I looked down at myself and instead of the t-shirt I knew I had been wearing, I was attired all in black, in a frock coat and stockings.

'All at once there was a fearful, triumphant yell from outside. "There he is – up there – see his shadow!"

'Suddenly there was a furious hammering on the door. I looked out of the little window that had so betrayed me again. The men outside had fetched axes and two were attacking the door while the others gazed evilly up at me, leering, their lips sneering, all the while taunting me, threatening me with what they proposed to do to me.

'It seemed an age, and yet an instant – the door, tough though it was, gave way under those crashing blows. The beasts ran in and up the spiral staircase towards me – I should say us. The woman in the room screamed, in French, but with a tremendous accent, "Help us, dear God! Husband, help us!" The children were screaming too, now.

'I found that I was holding a cocked pistol – I have no idea how it got there. Suddenly the door of the bedroom burst open and a monster of a man, swarthy, unshaven, carrying an axe, smashed his way in. I levelled the pistol at him and fired, catching him full in the chest. He instantly fell on the floor. I knew he was dead, though I don't know how I knew.

'There was a pause and silence – confusion. I realised that I had shot the leader. But quickly another man, smaller, but no less evil-looking, burst in and leaned over the body while others of the band slowly advanced, pointing swords and axes at me. I realised that, having discharged the pistol, I was defenceless. The newcomer leered up at me.

"So you killed him at last!"he shouted. "You killed me brother! But now I take revenge!"

'Without further word he leapt towards the woman and the children, his sword large and ugly in his hand. I threw myself forward to protect them, but he knocked me aside with a blow that I shall never forget. Then two of his henchmen pounced on me and grabbed me.

"You will watch this and then die, Hugo!" shouted my attacker, as he hacked at the pathetic group until they all lay dead on the tiled floor, their blood black in the candle-light.'

'This scene was so horrible, and so real, that I no longer believed I was part of the comfortable world of the 21st century, but that I had travelled through that cursed window into another time – into another person, another life.

'Every one of the gestures and moves that I made during that horrible time, every word that I said, seemed predestined – as if I, that is the conscious I sitting here now in this palace of modernity, had no will, nothing to do but to play a pre-determined role in an oft-repeated tragedy.

'Anyway I had little enough time to think as the rough hands that held me dragged – or perhaps threw – me down the stairs. Outside, the band encircled me and I could smell the drink on their breaths. I looked up and could see flames mounting inside the room I had so recently witnessed such awful things in.

'Then I saw him coming out – he who had murdered my wife and children – you see, I was now fully inhabiting this other life, this life that I had never known or dreamed of before – and I broke free from the arms that held me and leapt at him in a fury of rage. But he just laughed a sickening laugh of pure evil and sliced at me with his sword, cutting me under the chin and slitting my throat open. I fell to the ground, feeling my life's energy flood out onto the ground, and the scene around me faded to blackness.'

The physical effort that Jim had required to relate this astonishing tale had taken its toll on him and he lapsed into silence, his shoulders heaving, pale, the perspiration beaded on his forehead. Then he spoke again.

'My wife and children left as soon as they – well as soon as they could. I moved into a hotel and from there arranged for the house to go back on the market. I could not bring myself to go to the fat rogue who had sold us the place – I'm sure he knew something and that was why he had tried to put us off.

'In fact I had a bit of a job getting anyone to take it on their books. Apparently the house has a reputation. But eventually I found an agent, someone who deals mainly with foreigners. And before I left the place for the last time I had that infernal window plastered up, both inside and out.'


'One last thing,' said Jim, as we thought he had finished. 'Two days ago I went to the local museum to see if I could find out more, and I spoke to a historian who knew the house well.

'Apparently during the Revolution it was occupied by a Notary Public with Royalist sympathies. His family had been in a blood feud with a family from the next village for generations. One night two brothers of this clan gathered a band of ruffians to put an end to the feud, under the pretext of putting down a well known Royalist. The Notary and his wife and children, together with those servants who could not escape, were all massacred. But before he died the Notary shot and killed the older of the two brothers.' Jim sat back slowly.

'And there my story ends.'

'My God!' said the Glaswegian, at length breaking the shocked silence that we had all lapsed into. 'That's a hell of a yarn, Jim. But surely it was all just a bad dream brought on by the *coq* and too much Pommard? You must have heard the story of the blood feud somewhere and suggestion did the rest.'

Jim stared at him and then laughed a hollow laugh. 'I knew you wouldn't believe me,' he said quietly, and then, more firmly, 'You know I really do wish it were as simple as that. But then you should know that my wife found me in a dead faint in the road outside the house. That I was in a fever for days. I nearly died.

'And if that's not enough to convince you that what I experienced was more than a simple nightmare brought on by too much food and drink, then perhaps you'd like to explain this. If it was caused by a nightmare, then it's a different order of nightmare from any I've ever heard of.'

And so saying he quietly slipped off the cravat, to reveal a fiery red weal, looking like nothing so much as a recently healed gash, deeply cut into the flesh, which stretched quite from one ear to the other.

*This story is set at my own home in Burgundy, where I now live. There is indeed an échaugette and it did have a small window blocked up by a bathroom cabinet.*

*The action is loosely based on a true account of an attack on our village, which was Royalist, by Revolutionaries from the next village, in 1790. However, while the village Notary was taken prisoner he was not executed, thanks to the efforts of his wife.*

*There is a toilet in my little échaugette, and many times I have peered out of its tiny peep-holes at the street below; thankfully I have never seen a band of armed men intent on doing me harm!*

# *Imaginary Friends*

Bill and Angela Calder had first seen the old manse at Auchenlaw in the summer of 2008; but it was another four years before they had the opportunity to buy it.

This manse, like so many others, had long since become a civilian dwelling-house, we might say, but it retained its charm and its original Victorian features. It stood above the banks of Rescobie Loch in Angus. It was on north side of the loch, but in a sunny position, since the lowering whaleback of the hill beyond the loch never cast a shadow on the house, even in the depths of winter. The views from its windows, across the water and away to the south, were spectacular, to say the least.

The garden was bounded on the north, east and west by a mature beech hedge, which served as an effective windbreak. In that part of Scotland the icy blast from the north-east in winter, when the wind seems to carry with it the glacial heart of Siberia where it originated, would cut right through the heaviest garments, so this was definite advantage. There was a garage and numerous outbuildings. There was a fruit orchard, a vegetable garden and even a small wood.

All in all it was beautiful home, perfect for the couple and their young family.

The Calders had been buying and selling property for a decade even before they saw the Auchenlaw Manse for the first time. Their habit – not an unusual one – was to invest in an old property, refurbish it and then sell it on. By the time that the Manse came on the market in 2012, their capital was enough to secure it without even a mortgage. The timing was perfect; their previous house was already on the market and had interested parties ready to bid.

The Calders – who had fallen in love with the place on their first sight of it – lost no time. Am offer was placed and accepted; there is no need to go into more detail than that.


The house itself was in good condition, with no structural repair needed. While the decor was not much to their taste, that was an easy thing to fix.

The problem, for the Calders, was that, if anything, there was not enough to do.

Nevertheless, they bought the house and duly moved in. Repainting and repapering the walls and remodelling the kitchen (Angela Calder was very particular about kitchens) did not take them long, which left them scratching their heads for a project.

They decided to develop an area about ten metres square to the south of the house. It was a scruffy corner that had been neglected. However, there was already a door that gave straight onto it, and it would, they agreed, be a perfect place to watch the sunset from in summer. They would build a conservatory on part of it, with a paved area beyond. They could almost taste the gin martinis already.

The contractor that Calder had engaged sent a digger to scrape the topsoil and level the site. Soon after, the operator, a man of around thirty-five called Davie, stopped and knocked on the house door. Bill was in his study.

'You'd better come and have a look here, Mr Calder,' he said.

The operator led the way back to the site where he was excavating and showed Bill what he had found.

'There's been a building here before. Look.'

He showed how the whole area was filled in with bricks. 'Looks like it's been knocked in on itself,' he said.

'Yes it does, mused Bill. 'What do you think?'

'Well, I dug a track across here – there's definitely foundations, big ones. It looks to me like it's been a wing of the house.' He turned and looked at the gable. 'Pity it's been harled. Can't see the stonework.' He squinted. 'Wait...look there. You can see the a line in the masonry under the harling. It's been a roof. There's definitely been a wing here at some time in the past.'

Bill nodded. 'Funny, there's nothing in the drawings.'

'These are old bricks, Mr Calder. 19th century. Look.' He held one up. 'They haven't made bricks like that in over a hundred years.'

Again, Davie was right and Calder sucked a tooth. 'You know your stuff, I see,' he mused.

'Och, I've been doing this round here for twenty years. You see a lot of interesting things. And local history is kind of my hobby. These bricks came from a place near Dundee. Used to be a big brickworks there.'

'Fascinating. I wonder why they knocked it down.'

'People do funny things, Mr Calder. But this was a substantial building. These are big foundations. You just plan to put up a conservatory and slab the rest of the area?'

'Yes'.

'Ideal, then. I'll just scrape off the earth and level it out. Then we can spread out a hundred tonnes or so of hard-core and you can put whatever you want on top of it. We can deliver the hardcore the day after tomorrow. Have it done by the weekend.'

'Great! You just carry on then.'

The driver was as good as his word; he scraped off the topsoil, levelled the bricks and by the Friday afternoon, where once there had been a scruffy piece of wasteland, there was a nice levelled area ready to be slabbed.

The driver grinned as he got ready to depart. 'I'll have a snoop about and see if I can find out anything, Mr Calder, about what might have been there. There's maybe a record somewhere. We're a bit strapped just now with the harvest and the holidays coming on, but I'll have more time after that.'

There is no need to go into the details, here, of the rest of the work. The conservatory and patio were delightful.


The Calders had two children, both boys, Sam, aged four and Steven, aged seven. They shared a large room on the upper floor of the house that overlooked the new patio.

By the next summer, the family had established its routine in the new home. In Scotland, the summer evenings are long and wonderful; in June it stays light till eleven. The boys, of course, had to go to bed much earlier, at eight, as is right and proper for small children.

Once the stories had been read and the hugs and kisses dealt with, the curtains would be drawn and the boys told to sleep. Usually Bill and Angela would then potter around the house or garden until the light grew indigo and evening fell over the loch.

Once a week, usually on a Friday, however, they would go to Forfar for a few drinks. The town was not far and the taxi ride was only a few pounds. So they could have a fine evening and relax without worrying about having to drive.

Obviously, they couldn't leave the boys alone, so they hired – recommended through friends – a young girl from Forfar to babysit. The arrangement was that the taxi would be used both directions, once bringing the girl, Sandra Fairlie, to the Manse and taking the Calders to town and vice versa at the end of the evening. The driver would wait for five minutes while Angela briefed Sandra for the evening and then again, to hear any reports – which were few.

Sandra was a serious girl of sixteen. Once she had the boys settled, she would sit in the kitchen, where she would study – she was still at school – or watch television and relax and relax, her ear on the baby alarm. Once in a while she would slip up the stairs and just do a quick visual check that everything was as it should be, then return to the kitchen.

One night, as she was preparing to get into he taxi, Sandra said something to Angela.

'Oh, your boys. What wee scamps they are.'

'Why?'

'Oh I hear them chattering on the baby alarm but they must hear me, because whenever I get up to their room, there they are in their beds, for all the world as if they'd slept right through.

'Ah, thank you, Sandra,' said Angela, handing her her wages. 'Has this happened before?'

'Aye, a couple of times. But they're definitely getting bolder. Maybe they just can't sleep with the light nights. I was like that.'

Angela made a note to herself to investigate this and wished Sandra good night. The girl was clearly doing all she could; after all, you can't force children to sleep.

The more she thought about it though, the more it troubled her. She had noticed that the boys seemed lethargic and had been wondering if they were sickening with something; but if they were staying awake till midnight, then that might explain it.

She slipped silently up the stairs tot heir room and opened the door; there they both were, apparently fast asleep. She cleared her throat. They did not budge. Closing it behind her she went back downstairs to join Bill, who was pouring a couple of brandies.

'We'll need to keep an eye on that,' she said. 'Cheers.'

'Most likely as Sandra says – I remember the long nights when I was a child. So difficult to sleep, even with the curtains drawn.'

'Yes, well. I'm going to keep an eye on them from now on. They've both seemed so tired and...drained, lately.'

Bill nodded. 'Good idea.' He paused. 'There's something else I want to talk to you about.'

'What?' Angela sank in beside him on the sofa.

'Those damn cats.'

'Gosh yes. Where did they come from?'

'I don't know. You haven't been feeding them, have you?'

'No, and I cant get near them. Are they doing any harm?'

'I don't think so, but I don't want to encourage them.'

'Well all we can do is monitor it. If they start to breed we'll have to call in the Council or someone. You know what feral cats are like.'


Some days later, because it was raining, Angela had set the boys up an art project on the kitchen table. Passing, she glanced at Steven's painting. 'Who are those?' she asked, suddenly. 'Your cousins?

Steven shook his head.

'Well then, school friends? We can have some of your friends over if you like, it's a long summer holiday.'

'Oh, no, Mummy!'

'Really? I though you got on well with the Henderson boys.'

Steven shook his head, his jaw firm.

'Well then, who are these?' asked his mother, slightly exasperated. She glanced at her son and noticed what – fear? – in his eyes. Whatever it was, she didn't like it.

'Who are these children? Look, you've drawn them too.'

'Mummy I ...'

'Be quiet! You'll spoil it all. You know we're not supposed –'

'Not supposed to what?' demanded Angela, now worried. 'Sam? Steven? You tell me what this is about at once!'

'We're not supposed to tell you, Mummy!' blurted out Sam, teas welling in his eyes.

Steven swept his painting onto the floor.

'That's quite enough of your tantrums, Steven!'

'Now Sam – what are you not supposed to tell me? And who said this?'

'They're our friends.'

'Not any more they won't be!'

'Steven, that is enough! What friends, Sam?'

'They come to our room at night, Mummy.'

Angela could feel her heart freeze.

'They come to your room? And what do they do?'

'They –'

'Shut up, Sam!'

'That's enough, Steven! Go to your room at once!'

Steven stood up and went to the door. 'They told us not to say anything. You've spoiled it. I *hate* you!'

'Sam, what is all this about? Who are these children?'

'I don't know, Mummy. They only come at night. They live outside.'

'They live outside? What on earth do you mean?'

Angela glanced up at the kitchen window. There were four cats sitting on the sill, watching intently. 'Oh those bloody cats! Well, what do they do, these children?'

'They cuddle us.'

'Cuddle you?'

'Yes Mummy. They say they're cold. They only want to get warm.'

'And that's all they do?'

'Yes,' replied Sam, in a tone that made it clear to Angela that it was *not*.

'Samuel Calder, you tell me right now what they do!'

'Well, they kiss, Mummy.'

'Kiss?'

'Yes Mummy. But only on the neck. Just here.'

Angela looked. she could see no mark. She shook her head. Nightmares. The children must be having nightmares. But why?

Sam was looking at her, his bottom lip trembling. 'Am I in trouble, Mummy?'

'Oh goodness me, no, darling, of course not.' Angela hugged him, feeling her own tears well up. 'Of course not. But do you think I could meet these children?'

'No. They won't let you. They won't let you near them.' At this the boy's eyes swivelled to the window. Sheila glanced round too.

'Wait a minute...have you been letting these cats into your bedroom?'

'I didn't let them in! I promise, Mummy!'

'Well, who does?'

'Steven. But he says we must never, ever tell or you'll stop them coming.'

Angela could not think whether to laugh or cry.

'So these are cats?'

Sam nodded.

'So why are they children in your drawing?'

'Because they're children too, Mummy.' Samuel shrugged.

'They're cats...*and* they're children?'

'Yes, Mummy.'

Angela sat down heavily. This was a very peculiar nightmare.

'And they come every night?'

'Yes Mummy. Every night.'


Angela found her husband in his study, reading some contract papers.

'Bill?'

'Yes, love.'

'Ummm...tell me, did you ever have an imaginary friend when you were a child?'

Calder looked up quickly. 'Gosh, yes. Didn't I ever tell you?'

'No. I mean it's common enough, isn't it?'

'I daresay. I never really gave it much thought.'

'What do you remember?'

'It was a long time ago, Angela. About all I can tell you is that he was a boy called Rusty.'

'Your parents knew about him?'

'My mother did, for sure. I remember talking to her about him. And my pony...they wanted to call him Rusty but I wouldn't let them. So I suppose Dad must have known too.'

'What happened to him?

'When my brother was born he just vanished. That was it. Never saw him again.'

'And you really saw him?'

'Oh yes, as plain as you are right now.'

'So did you talk to him?'

'All the time. That was how Mum found out I think. She kept asking who I was talking to.'

'But she never saw him.'

'Of course not. He made himself invisible when there were others around. I was the only one who could see him.'

Angela just stared at her husband. 'So this, this imaginary friend...he was real, to you?'

'Angela,' replied Bill, slowly. 'Angela, he *was real*. I don't know what he was, but he was real. He was there, with me. All the time. Never left my side.'

'But he was invisible sometimes.'

Bill thought about that a moment. 'Not to me. I could always see him. But I know that the others couldn't and that somehow he made it that way. But he was with me all the time.'

'You surely don't mean in a physical sense?'

'Oh, as an educated adult, I have to say no, I suppose not... but for me then, and for my inner whatever, soul, being, I don't know, right now – yes he *was* physically real. I mean he could do things and make them happen. We would play games together and he would, you know, play. He was very active.'

'What did he look like?'

Bill shrugged. 'I can't see his face, now. He was a little boy like me. But with curly fair hair, and mine was straight.'

'And did he ever...uh, did he ever appear in another form?'

'What do you mean?'

'Like as an animal…maybe a cat, say?'

'Gosh, no. He wasn't a shape-shifter, if that's what you mean.' Bill looked hard at Angela. 'What's all this about, love? Don't tell me *you've* got one now?'

'No, but the boys might have, I think.'


Angela looked out from the conservatory. The day was grey and cloudy. In front of her was the new patio area that had been laid with slabs. But she was not admiring what was, admittedly, a fine piece of work. She was watching Sam and Steven. They were in the southeast corner of the patio, talking earnestly, but not to each other. They seemed, from the inclination of their heads and their body language, to be talking to a group of other children.

But there were no children there. Instead, Angela could see four cats. They were just sitting on the ground, looking at the boys. There was something that Angela didn't like about it and she made for the door.

'Boys! Boys, come inside and leave those filthy cats. They're strays, they'll be full of fleas.' She crossed the patio towards them but the cats did not at first run; instead they arched their backs and hissed at her, their eyes flaming with hatred. Only at the last moment did they break and run.

'We're going to have to do something about those bloody cats,' she said to herself.


Bill was taking his morning coffee on the lovely new patio. The sun was already high and it was warm. 'Going to be a roaster,' he said to himself, putting down his newspaper. He cast his eyes over the nice, new, paved area. Around it, there was a low wall, built on the foundations of the old wing. It had a steel gate, so that the children could play in the patio without escaping into the wider world beyond. His eyes narrowed.

'Hello, what's that? Looks like some of those slabs have moved.'

He rose and crossed to the southeast corner of the patio. Sure enough, there was a problem with the paving. The slabs appeared to have subsided and there was a depression about two metres across.

The builder arrived at eleven, after a brief conversation on the phone.

'It's definitely subsided,' said Bill, while the builder scratched his head and sucked a tooth. 'I thought you had tamped this all down.'

'Aye we did, sir, and consolidated it with a whacker. You remember, you saw us. And all this,' he stamped his foot, 'Is on a thick layer of brick with eight inches of hardcore over it. I don't understand.'

'There are no mines around here, are there?'

'Oh no, Mr Calder. None. I've never seen a case of subsidence in this area, not in twenty years.'

'That's what I thought.'

'Well, we'll come and dig that out and see if we can fix it. I'm sorry about all this.'

'So am I,' replied Bill, dryly. 'Can you get a digger in?'

'No, we'll have to do it by hand. I'm tight for staff though, with holidays coming up.'

'Well, it needs to be done. A person could trip on this and break their damn neck.'

'Aye, Mr Calder. I suspect there's a problem with drains. Subsidence is usually drains. Look, I tell you what: I'll put Jack and Eric on it. Jack's an older man so he can't really do any hard work, but there's nothing in the building trade he doesn't know. I have every confidence in him. And Eric, well, Eric's very good at digging.'


Sure enough, the next morning at 8 am sharp, they arrived. Jack was, as had been promised, an older man, who quickly reassured Calder with the breadth of his knowledge. While his assistant, the doughty Eric, was unloading the tools, Jack did something that surprised Calder. Taking a bent piece of wire in each hand, he began criss-crossing the area where the slabs had settled. The wires were bent into elongated 'L' shapes, so that with the foot in his hand, the long part protruded horizontally before him about ten inches.

Calder watched, fascinated: every time Jack stepped on the

suspect area, the wires flicked so that they were crossed.

'I've never actually seen that done,' he said to Jack.

'Aye, my dad taught me. It's s gift, really. Mr Calder, I don't know what's down there. I've never felt something so strong. It's maybe a well or something. It's big, anyway. We'll have to lift all those slabs and the ones around, then Eric can dig down and we can do some investigating.'

'If it is a well?'

'I'd be getting a bowser of concrete in and just fill it up, sir.'

Calder chuckled. 'My thoughts exactly.'

Within an hour the slabs were up and Eric was manfully attacking the layers below. Digging up hardcore and broken brick by hand is fiendish work, but he didn't seem to mind. All Jack – whose role was clearly supervisory – would say, when Calder asked, was, 'Aye, Eric likes to dig. Don't you, Eric?'

To which there was an affirmative grunt.

The men broke for lunch at twelve and returned at one. By then the full heat of the day was blazing down on the patio, which was a real sun-trap. But this did not seem to affect Eric's progress.

By five, a significant hole had been dug, but nothing discovered as yet.

Saying only 'There's something down there, I know it,' Jack promised to return in the morning and continue.


That night, Angela put he boys to bed at eight as usual. She and Bill watched television for a while together. Just as it became dark, Angela became aware of the sound of voices coning from the baby alarm. Children's voices.

'Oh those boys,' she exclaimed. 'I told them to go to sleep hours ago.' Angela sprang up the stairs towards the fist floor, but they seemed to telescope out ahead of her, as if she were in a nightmare. The higher she climbed, the further away seemed the landing. Infuriated, she redoubled her efforts and, panting, made it. But now everything as in slow-motion. She tried to hurry towards the boys' room, but it took an age. And when she arrived she heard something that made her blood run cold.

She could hear not two voices, but many, all talking at once. There were people in there with the children! She threw herself against he door, but it had jammed. It had never done that before. No matter how hard she shoved it refused to give. It was if it were locked or bolted.

'Not my babies! Don't harm my babies!' she yelled aloud and suddenly the door flew open.

She was not prepared for what she saw. The boys were lying in their beds. On top of each were two cats. They had their mouths on the boys' necks and they were massaging them with their forepaws. As Angela entered, they looked up from their filthy task. She could clearly see the blood on their mouths and streaming from her sons' necks. As she realised what she was seeing, the cats leapt straight at her, screaming with hellish fury. She recoiled, her mouth wide in terror.

Suddenly the room lights came on and someone pushed Angela aside. He threw a handful of grey powder at the cats, who howled fiendishly – and then disappeared. Angela fell backwards in shock and was caught by Bill, who was right behind her. With him were Jack and Davie, the digger-driver. Jack was holding a bucket.

'Wood ash,' he said. 'I mind reading somewhere that it might work.'

But here was no time to waste in further explanations.

'We must help the children,' he said. 'Quickly now!'

Despite the noise and confusion, the boys lay still and pale as corpses. Angela screamed and rushed towards them.

'No, Mrs Calder,' exclaimed Jack, catching her. 'They're not dead. But only you can bring them back. You must call them.'

'Call them?'

'Do you not realise what you have just seen? Those are vampires. They've been feeding on your children for months. But they didn't kill them. Tonight they intended to suck their blood dry and turn them into vampires too.'

'But why?'

'Because we uncovered their lair. The only thing that can save them is their mother's love. Yours is the most pure love of all. Close your eyes now and do as I say.'

Angela closed her eyes, still shaking.

'Open your mind's eye. Do you see them?'

'Yes... they're lying there, looking at me.'

'Call them to you. Call them now.'

Her mouth dry as the wood-ash, Angela called her sons and they rose, like sleepwalkers, from their beds. When they came to her she could hold her emotions no longer; she threw her arms around them and burst into tears.

With that the spell was broken and they came awake, their eyes blinking.

'Mummy, I had a terrible dream,' said Steven.

There was not a mark on either and of cats, there was no sign.


Later, with the boys tucked up in a shakedown on the sofa, the four adults shared a whisky.

'We'll be staying here tonight,' said Jack. 'They won't come back, but we shall not leave the house until daylight. Meantime, we are under your protection, Mrs Calder.'

'Me?'

'Yes. You're a mother. They can't fight the power of a mother's love and they know who and what you are now. They'll not challenge you again. You have wielded your power to bring your own children back from a ghastly eternity of half-life. They know your power. They fear it.'

'How did you know?'

'I knew there was something evil in that hole,' said Jack. 'But when Davie came round to me tonight I realised what it was.'

Davie took up the story. 'I did a bit of research, Mrs Calder. In the 1890s there were some funny goings-on round here. Four children disappeared in Forfar. There was nothing to connect them and their bodies were never found. Local wisdom had it that they must have drowned in the loch.

'Shortly after that, a new wing was built out to the east of the house here, as we thought. After the owners who built it died, the new ones never had any end to bother with it. Apparently the walls kept cracking. Eventually they knocked the whole thing in on itself and left it that way.'

'And then I came and built on it again,' interjected Calder.

'Aye, but you were not to know,' replied Jack. 'Tomorrow Davie and I will finish excavating what's out there. I think it might be a grim task.'


As soon as it was light, but before the sun had risen, Bill Calder, Davie and Jack made their way out. Nobody had slept a wink. It didn't take long to find what they were looking for. A big stone flag had been laid, but it had been broken.

'You probably cracked it with the digger,' noted Jack, to Davie. 'Easy done. That's what must have caused the subsidence. And wakened whatever lies under it.'

'Aye, but what *is* under it?'

'We'll find out soon enough. But I'm not thinking it's going to be a well.'

Using a pair of long crows, they levered up the edge of the largest part of the slab and flipped it over.

'*Oh, my God!*' exclaimed Calder.

In the grave were the perfectly-preserved bodies of four children. Their eyes were closed but their hands were raised to chest level; their fingernails were broken and the blood was still red and fresh. Calder moved forward

'No, sir!' exclaimed Jack, holding him back. 'You can't help them!'

As he spoke, the dead eyes of all four flicked open and the men recoiled as the bodies sat up; but at that moment the sun breasted the hill on the other side of the loch and a finger of golden light fell on them.

The thee men watched in horror as the apparitions before them writhed in the burning sun, before crumpling back down into the grave and disappearing. And then all that was left were four pathetic, long-forgotten skeletons.

Jack shook his head. 'Poor wee things. Well, that solves one mystery.' He looked at the others. 'We'll have to notify the police. Let's make sure we have the story straight. We tell them exactly what happened, except for the parts about the cats and your children, and what we just saw. Davie broke the slabs with his digger, they collapsed on the grave and that is how we found it. Okay?' The others nodded and Jack went to the van.

When he returned a few moments later, had with him a tarpaulin, which he spread over the grave.

The bodies, after due process of investigation, were buried in Forfar. Their sad grave at the manse was filled in with concrete, and never again did the patio slabs move.

Of bloodsucking cats or imaginary friends, nobody saw or heard another thing, ever again. But still, the Calders, soon afterwards, put Auchenlaw Manse on the market; they hoped to make a decent profit.

*Shape-shifting creatures of a wide variety are a feature of Scottish folklore; we have water-horses, seals (selkies), hares and other beasts who are known to be human part of the time and become animals when it suits their business to do so. Cats seemed to be an appropriate and interesting variation on a theme.*

*The idea of shape-shifting beasts is ancient. Prince Vlad Dracul, 'Dracula' was a Wallachian hero who defended his country from the Ottoman Turks in the 15th century. Famously, Prince Vlad held a banquet for the Ottoman nobles, their wives and children, and when they were trapped in his castle, had them all impaled on wooden spikes. This became something of a passion for him and he gained the name 'Vlad the Impaler'. His bloodthirsty ways led to his being associated with vampires, which were blood-sucking shape-shifters that could not be killed.*

*It is possible that Prince Vlad himself encouraged these myths in order to strike terror into his enemies; such early terror-propaganda was used elsewhere, especially by the Spanish, to frighten conquered popualtions into submission.*

*However, both impalement and blood-sucking shape-shifters go back much further. Impalement was used in much of the ancient world, notably Egypt.*

*Blood-sucking winged creatures of the night can be traced to Sumerian times. One was the 'lilitu', a creature who appeared similar to a woman but with wings and a vulture's feet, who sucked unborn babies from the wombs of their mothers.*

John Grant could never remember where or how he had picked up the habit of rummaging through junkshops and flea-market stalls.

He was not a wealthy man, though he was well educated and comfortable. He held a part-time job as a lecturer in Art History, and this allowed him enough to have a small but cosy flat, a car, to eat and drink moderately well, and to indulge his habit of hunting for treasure in these dusty places.

Grant was lightly built, but tall, with grey-blue eyes and fair hair; his middle already, even in his early thirties, had begun to show the first signs of a paunch brought on by an over-fondness for good Edinburgh ale, which any but an Englishman knows to be the finest in the world.

His job – or rather his Professor – demanded a certain maintenance of standards of dress, but Grant's salary did not run to the purchase of expensive suits. So in dress he tended to the sober and practical, sports jackets and slacks. His car was second-hand and prone to giving trouble, but since he rarely used it, preferring to walk to work, this was not such a great difficulty.

You might have taken John Grant for any one of those who, having taken their doctorates, find themselves with their feet on the first rungs of the academic ladder, for want of anything better to do; not overly cursed with either imagination or ambition, but with intelligence aplenty and the common sense to be deferential when occasion requires it.

He was still unmarried, for though a number of women had hove up close over the years, John Grant had found himself not ready to make a deep commitment. And so they had passed from his life, usually peacefully, sometimes not. Recently he had struck up with a woman who taught at another university. She had taken to coming to Edinburgh to pass weekends with him.

Other than this he had been living as he now did for two years, alone, in his little flat in Edinburgh's Marchmont, letting his life meander and enjoying his small pleasures; visiting the pub at the corner two or three times a week, going for walks in the Meadows, which he loved, especially in spring; an occasional meal at an Indian restaurant with friends; but most of all rooting and snuffling through the piles in the city's junkshops.

The year had begun like any other; dark and wet winter had passed into the rawness of March, and now April was no more and May was begun, filled with warm eddies of scented breezes that held the promise of summer.

One such afternoon Grant left his place of gainful employ and turned his path eastwards towards Causewayside, meaning to idle an hour or so in the junkshops there. His searches were at first fruitless; though there were, as always, many things to delight and to interest, he never felt that quickening, that thrill which spurred him to buy.

So he had decided to make his way home, when he turned a corner and there, before him was that most wonderful of enticements, a new shop, filled with who knew what treasure. Without any hesitation at all, Grant swung the door open. Somewhere in the dim recess of the back shop a bell rang, and he could hear the sounds of movement.

As his eyes grew used to the gloom which is customary in establishments of this sort, he realised that he was gazing at rows and rows of books. The shop was more an antiquarian bookseller than general *bric-a-brac*; but since he was passionately interested in books, this was of no matter at all, and he eagerly began to scour the shelves of leather spined books.

Mostly they were old novels of little interest and a few geographical treatises. He lingered a while on a beautiful leather-bound Burckhardt, before deciding that the asking price was too steep, and anyway he had a copy; indeed he was on the point of sighing and leaving without dipping his hand into his pocket, when his eye was caught by a small volume, leather bound again, and very old.

He drew it carefully from the shelf and felt a tingle of anticipation that was almost a physical sensation. Now this was more like it! The book was, he discovered on close examination, a Bible, which had been printed in the year 1700. The script was peculiar and hard to read, with many of the 's's' appearing as 'f's' after the ancient style, but the book was clearly an item of value.

The leather binding, even after serving two hundred years, was still in good condition, though much scuffed and bent on the corners. The spine was broken in several places, but the stitching still held, and no pages were missing. The pages themselves were a beautiful wove vellum, which were mostly dog-eared and showed many stains and marks.

The price was pencilled in at the top right hand corner of the flyleaf. When he saw it John Grant knew that he had struck gold; he had found his bargain for the day. The seller only wanted three pounds for the book! It was so obviously a bargain, even in the state it was in, that it was laughable.

Grant turned, clutching the book, and looked for the shopkeeper, who had moved out of the back shop almost silently. He now stood by the counter, gazing out of the window in the manner of one who wishes to observe you, but who does not wish to seem to be doing so.

He smiled when Grant approached; a thin man, wearing a cardigan, slightly balding, unremarkable. Yet – there was something in his manner; he seemed as if an oppression lay upon him. He seemed weary and certainly looked as if he could have done with a good night's sleep. No – it was more than that – there was something, something in his eyes, something unpleasant, as if they had seen too much of the worse side of life. But though he remarked this, it was no matter to Grant, who only wanted to buy a book.

'Have you found something, sir?'

'Yes I have. This,' replied Grant, handing over the book.

'Ah, indeed. *That* one.'

Did the man pale? Surely not. Whatever, he handed it back to John quickly enough. But then he *did* shake himself, so that Grant could not but notice.

'Are you all right?'

'Oh yes, sir. Bit of a draught, that's all. Now that will be three pounds, I believe.'

Grant was startled. There were thousands of books in the shop, and to know the price of each – it was impossible. And yet the man had definitely not looked at the flyleaf.

Grant rummaged in his trouser pocket and fished out three coins. He handed them to the shopkeeper, who grasped them quickly and held them.

'A bargain that,' said Grant, feeling, now that the sale was transacted, that he could show off a bit. 'It's eighteenth century – hand printed.'

'A bargain? Oh. Och, well, you know, it's been – it's been for sale a while, you know. Got to keep the stock moving, can't have it on the shelves too long.'

Now this was a preposterous statement on the part of a dealer like this. Ordinarily Grant would have made some remark, especially as he was quite sure that the shop had not even been there when last he had passed this way only two weeks before, but a queer look on the man's face told him that no more would be said.

'Will that be all, sir?'

'Yes, thank you. Goodbye.' Grant left the shop, and was struck by the impression that the man was almost willing him to leave; and as he let the door swing behind him, he could have sworn that he heard a sigh – a sigh of relief, he could only wonder, and then a low chuckle before the door swung to. He walked away up the street, and at the corner looked back. The blinds on the shop had been drawn.

He shrugged, and thought to himself that the man must have decided to take the afternoon off; though three pounds was hardly cause for celebration. He wouldn't go far in business with an attitude like that. And he had not even offered to wrap the book – surely a little odd? But Grant thought little of it; the owners of antiquarian bookshops and the like were well known to be an eccentric bunch, and it would not have been the first time that he had been startled by their manners.

Grant made his way to the centre of the Meadows, past occasional groups of lads diligently practising their golf swings. He found a convenient bench under one of the cherry-blossom trees and sat down to look at his prize. What a handsome piece! In the sunlight the deep brown of the leather seemed as serene as it must have been when the book was new; it just invited the hand to run over it, and it felt smooth and supple. The gold lettering on the spine was bright, and perfectly formed, with no worn patches. It must have been more gloomy than he had thought in that shop, as he clearly remembered having had to strain his eyes to pick out those same letters when he had first picked up the book. And hadn't it looked more dull, more grimy? It was wonderful what the sunlight could do. Now he could make out a faint design on the spine that he had not even noticed before, and which he was sure would respond to a little gentle cleaning.

He opened the cover to look for an inscription – he had been so keen to buy the thing that he hadn't looked before. Sure enough there was something, written in a hand that had not been used for many years. The writing was so faded, however, that Grant could not make out what it said, except for the date, which was 1701. This tallied nicely with the legend on the flyleaf, which said that it had been printed by J&W Eddowes for T Cadell and W Davies of The Strand, London, in 1700.

Having some time to idle away to himself, Grant flicked through the pages of his recent trophy. The writing was difficult to decipher, for the style of the lettering was archaic and, as well as this, the ink was in many places a little smudged. He had to study the words with great care to understand what they said.

He pored intently over the book, not coherently reading it, but rather dipping into passages, until he read, 'The hour of prayer is approaching, and I cannot reach home in time to perform my ablutions.' Just as he read this, Grant heard the bell of the university clock ring out seven and realised with a surprise how late it was. He laughed and slipped the book into his pocket. 'And how right you are,' he said to himself. 'I won't have time to go home; I'll be late.'

Very amused by this, he struck off over the Meadows in the direction of a well-known public house, where he had arranged to meet a friend.

Now it was a curious thing, but John Grant forgot all about the book when he met his friend. Throughout the evening – they had planned to have a drink and then go for a curry – it remained in his pocket unmentioned. It was not until he returned to his flat sometime after eleven that he remembered it, and he ticked himself off for being so remiss as to forget. His friend was also a collector of books and would, he was sure, have been interested in the little curiosity.

Grant was in a contented state as he entered his flat. He made coffee, and while waiting began to look at his Bible again. Then he remembered that because he had not had time to come home earlier, he had not checked the day's mail. He knew that there were important letters to come concerning an investment opportunity that he had been offered.

An old friend had made a proposition to him that was financially interesting but required a fair investment up front, and the letter would explain the details. He had been disinclined to take up the offer, though it seemed sound enough, because it would mean investing the whole of his savings. But he had just been reading a passage in his Bible that explained how a merchant, being required to pay out money, needed to borrow; and that not only had the merchant been successful, but the lender had refused to have the money back at the end of the loan.

Grant thought about this and then nodded; if the investment worked out then he could have pay his double-glazing several times over, so he would take the chance after all.

So, the next day, he sent off a cheque to his friend.


We shall skip over the next two months until the day when Grant received another letter, again from his friend. This explained that the deal had worked out as planned; if anything the profit had been even more than expected.

A cheque could be sent out by the end of the month, which Grant was delighted to see would repay his investment and much more; indeed he would see his original sum multiplied several times. However, in the letter his friend asked him to leave his money invested.

Naturally Grant was delighted by this good news, and he glanced up at his bookcase. There he saw the little leather-bound Bible that had given him such sound advice. He realised with a start that since that night he had not touched it at all, except to put it there in the case. Putting down the letter, he got up and picked the book out of the shelf.

'Thank you, little friend,' he murmured, 'Thank you very much indeed.' But what was this? The design on the spine of the book, which he had been quite faded when he had looked at it that bright day in the Meadows, was now almost as bright as the lettering of the title, which nowa ppeared as splendid as the day it had been done.

How curious, he thought, but he shrugged it off. Then he sat down with the book and opened it. The legend inscribed on the inside cover was still faint, but now he could actually read some of it.

'Who would have knowledge may dip within,' and then followed several more words, which Grant still could not decipher. The writing was formed in two lines, most of the first being legible and the second obscure. Then there were some other letters, which Grant took to be initials, and then the date.

Well, now this was a queer thing; only a matter of two months ago he had been unable to make out writing that was now clear as day; what could it mean? All he could think of was that perhaps the book had been a little damp, and the atmosphere of his flat had dried it out; yes that must be it…The central heating did make the air very dry. But he had not heard of that phenomenon before, and made a mental note to ask someone about it.

He sat down again, and realised that he had taken the book with him. But he thought he might look at it again, so he placed it on his desk before going on to read the rest of the letter from his friend.

It seemed that another company had an interest in some property that his friend's company owned, and which Grant had invested in so successfully. Apparently this other company was seeking to lever them out by disputing the title and had hired some very sharp lawyers. However, his friend was sure that if they could just hold on a little longer they would all be very wealthy. Grant sighed and put down the letter.

Again, he felt the chill of a decision being forced upon him. His friend had done very well by him, but he had heard some tales about the property market that made him unsure. He glanced up and saw that the Bible on his desk was open – well of course, he had been looking at the inscription – but it was no longer open there. I

nstead it had fallen open at page four hundred and sixty five, and the first passage that Grant saw was Chronicles 20:12, 'we have no might against this great company that cometh against us.'

'Well, that settles it,' he said to himself. 'You were right enough the first time, and I won't doubt you now.' And so he wrote a letter back to his friend refusing the request to invest further and asking for his cheque by return.

Once he had finished the letter, he picked up the Bible – closed this time. His fingers ran over the leather of the cover. It was sensuous, so tactile – so warm to the touch – he could hardly help himself but to stroke it gently with his fingertips.

An amusing thought struck him; here he was, a genuinely lapsed Christian who had not been to a church service, saving weddings and funerals, for nearly twenty years, stroking the cover of a Bible and referring to it as his 'little friend.' Ridiculous, quite ridiculous! And so, laughing, he got up and put the Bible back into the shelf.


That night Grant slept badly. He was troubled by dreams that he could only remember part of the next morning. He seemed to be on trial, protesting his innocence, shouting it at the top of his voice, but to no avail, for no-one seemed to listen; they – those others in his dream – just went about the remorseless business of legal procedure, paying no heed to him at all.

Several times he saw the face of his friend, his finger outstretched, as if accusing; but he could remember nothing of what was said to him, or why he was on trial. When he woke, he looked for the letter he had written, thinking that he night reconsider.

He could see now that there had been a hint of pleading in his tone; reading between the lines it seemed as if his friend might need Grant's invested money to win the fight he was engaged in. But it was too late, he remembered, as he scoured his desk; of course, he had posted the letter as he had walked to the pub the night before.

'Ah well, what's done is done,' he said to himself. But then something struck him: 'That's strange,' he thought, 'I'd completely forgotten that I went down to the pub last night.'

And more, his memory of the excursion was very vague indeed. Now John Grant was fond of a pint, and had been known to overdo the pleasure on occasion; but he really was not a hard drinker, and it was very unlike him to drink to excess – certainly not to the point of his memory being confused – during the week, because he had a horror of going to work with a hangover.

There was another strange thing; this morning he had not a trace of a hangover, and instead felt clear as a bell. Checking his wallet, he found that he could at most have had two pints of beer to drink, which was his usual for a midweek refreshment. But he shrugged his shoulders. 'Must be age,' he thought.

Within a few days a cheque duly arrived, with a very brief note from his friend saying that he was pleased that Grant had done so well, that he was sorry that he did not feel able to go on to greater things; but there it was, and so on, and wishing him luck.

Grant paid the cheque into his bank and thought little more about it.

But he did notice that his luck had changed.


Now, John Grant had never been a gambler; he had been brought up in the Presbyterian tradition to believe that gambling was immoral. In fact the sum of his gambling had been to buy a book of tickets from the department secretary for the Christmas raffle. The most he'd ever won was a half bottle of vodka, which, since he didn't like vodka, had been no win at all.

One day, however, a colleague asked him if he'd like to pay a visit to the races at Musselburgh that afternoon. Grant had never been to the races, so he agreed. It was a sunny afternoon and the idea tickled him. They drove down in his friend's car.

When it came time to bet on the first race, John's ignorance of the detail of betting made his friend laugh out loud. He had no knowledge of form or of the importance of the conditions, none of the skills which the horse-fancier thrives on. He just looked at the list of runners for the first race, and there was Bible John at eleven to one; so he asked his friend to put twenty pounds on it for him.

'To win?' asked his friend, and then had to explain what an each way bet was. But John put it on to win, and ten minutes later amazed his friend, who had put a tenner each way on the three to one favourite that had trailed home, by being £220 better off.

By the end of the day, John was up four figures and his friend had started backing the horses he picked.

'I must bring you racing again,' muttered his mentor. 'I've never seen beginner's luck like it.'


And then, not long after, a senior lecturer in his department, who was famed for his absent-minded behaviour, capped a career of careless accidents when he stepped out in front of a Number 10a and rendered closed his account of life on this earth. Grant couldn't help himself but to reflect on how very fortuitous this was; indeed he had frequently imagined just such an end to the old goat.

Very shortly afterwards the Professor buttonholed Grant in a corridor and quietly explained that he ought to apply for the vacant post; which of course Grant had been planning to do. In due course he was offered a contract as Senior Lecturer, which he was pleased to accept by return.

At the same time his private life was looking rosier than it had for years. His relationship with Fiona Barton was blossoming, and most weekends now either he travelled to Glasgow to be with her, or, as was more often the case, she came to pass the time in Edinburgh with him. In fact she had suggested that she might begin to look for a post in Edinburgh after the summer break, an idea which naturally pleased Grant.

His visits to the race course had continued: though he never repeated the amazing luck of his first day, his success was still surprising, and he was always a few hundred pounds up at the end of the day.

He began to dabble in the stock market, and here again, after a freakishly lucky start, settled down to a consistent level of successful investment that surprised and delighted his stockbroker.

As the summer months trickled by, friends who had known Grant for a long time began to comment; he had never been ostentatious, rather dowdy in fact; but now he dressed with style. He developed a taste for Italian shoes and sports jackets; he sold his old used car and bought a brand new one. He began to patronise a better class of restaurant, and frequently at that. He never lacked for company, for he was a generous drinker, always with his hand in his pocket.

There were other things, too. He began to change physically. He put on weight, around his middle at first, but it was soon followed by a fleshing out around the jowls. Grant was lightly built, so this became obvious quickly. And something that he could not quite define was happening to his eyes – the wrinkles were more pronounced, but the skin under them seemed to sag, as if he needed more sleep; but in fact he felt that he had never slept better in his whole life.

Not everything in Grant's life was rosy; there was a smell of damp in the living-room of his flat. Fiona, who viewed Grant's bachelor lifestyle somewhat less brightly than the man himself, had been the first to notice it. She flung open all the enormous Georgian sash windows that lit the room. That helped, but as soon as she left and Grant closed the windows, it came back again.

He began to suspect that roof repairs might be needed; but when he called in a firm of specialists to survey the roof, they could find no fault with it.

It was odd that he had never noticed this before, he told himself; but then he had become so much more fussy recently. Little details like that, which he formerly would have been oblivious to, had begun to niggle him.

Perhaps he should consider selling the flat and buying something a little bigger; perhaps a house in its own grounds in the Grange. His salary as a senior lecturer, together with his income from the stock market and the price he should get for his flat, should bring this within his reach.

Now only six months previously, Grant was entirely happy in his comfortable flat, and had thought it unlikely that he would ever move. The thought of buying a house in the price range he was now considering would have scared him so much that he'd have had to go for a few beers to help him forget the idea. But just as soon as he was struck by the idea of 'moving up the property ladder', he arranged an interview with his bank manager and began to scour the property pages. After all, he reasoned to himself, perhaps Fiona would move in – he did enjoy her company.

The bank manager was dubious; he did not believe that he could count the income from the stock market towards a mortgage, and this would leave Grant considerably short of the sum he would require to buy into the price band he wanted to. He was sorry, but...

Grant left the interview feeling depressed and grimly pondered what he would do to that bank manager if he could.

Of an evening Grant would often pass by the corner of his bookcase where the Bible was kept. It was a very gloomy corner, and nothing he did seemed to make any difference. If he changed the bulbs in the light fitting, they seemed to make the shadows there deeper, by making the rest of the room brighter.

That night he sat at his desk and went through his calculations again. No matter which way he looked at it, if the finicky old sod wouldn't take part of his income into account, he could not proceed with his plans. He looked up. It was late and the room was in darkness except for the lamp on his desk; the shadowy corner of the room where the bookcase stood was even more gloomy than usual, or so it seemed.

He rubbed his eyes. The darkest part of the shadow was where the Bible was kept and the shadow there seemed velvety black, like a hole into a deep void of darkest moonlit night. It seemed to have clouds moving within it, though Grant could rather sense them than see them, and every so often it appeared as if an eddy of darkness spiralled out from the inky centre and spread over the rest of the corner.

'Ridiculous,' muttered Grant to himself, crossing to the bookcase and retrieving the Bible. It really was a beautiful book, he thought, and rubbed the spine reflectively. And it was in such good condition.

Sitting down at his desk again, he opened the book and began to read. It seemed such a long time since he had dipped into it; yet it was always somehow reassuring. It was as if the words carried a real significance to his own life; and Grant, who was no religious man, thought this ironical.

How long had it been since he had read it? Well, he had read up to his page-mark, he knew, and then started, for the page-mark was at Jeremiah 31, which is halfway through.

'Why, I don't remember reading all of that,' he said to himself, and then, after flicking back through the pages and seeing that everything he read up to that point was familiar to him, he realised that he must have.

Not only must he have read the words, he must have studied them carefully, for no matter where he put his finger he found that he remembered exactly the phrase that was written there, and if he closed his eyes, could repeat the words aloud with never a mistake.

Now that was too odd, he reasoned. He remembered that his mother had sat him on her knee by the window every day as they waited for his father to come home from work, and read from the Bible. Perhaps by some queer subconscious process the words had fixed themselves in his memory and the book simply acted as a trigger.

He returned, pondering, to his page-mark and began to read again.


Two days later came drastic news. His father had died suddenly. This, naturally, was a great shock to Grant, even though he had not spoken to the old man in some time. He had always been closer to his mother and this had become more pronounced recently; his father resented gambling and regarded the playing of the stock market as little better.

Fiona accompanied him to the funeral. It was the first chance she had had to meet his mother and she was distraught never to have met his father. Indeed it seemed to Grant that she was more upset than he was. After all, his father had been over eighty. He had come into fatherhood late in life, which perhaps accounts for the distance between himself and his son.

But there was a silver lining to this, as to other clouds; his father had left a considerable sum of money – more than Grant had ever imagined – and while providing for his wife had still been able to leave to Grant, his only son, a six-figure sum; exactly, indeed, the amount Grant required to go ahead with his house-purchase plans.

As they drove back to Edinburgh after the funeral, which had taken place in Grant's home town of Broughton in the Scottish borders, Fiona said something which struck Grant as strange. She had been silent for most of the journey, and then at last turned to him.

'What is it, John,' she asked, with tears in her eyes. 'Have you got bored with me?'

Grant was taken aback. 'No, certainly not. Why did you say that?'

'Oh, I don't know…John, you never phone these days, and you used to, all the time, when we first started going out. You never say how I look, and you never….Oh! Never mind! But, John, sometimes you seem so cold, so calculating….I never thought that you were like that; when your mother told you about the Will, I could see – John, you *smiled!*'

'I'm sorry – It's just that – well, I suppose I'd better tell you –'

'What?'

'Well, I'd been thinking about buying a bigger place….a house in the Grange maybe. And I just thought – well, I thought that Dad's money would make that possible, and that would have pleased him.' This last was a lie; his father totally disapproved of ostentation.

'A house in the Grange?' cried Fiona incredulously. 'What for? You have a beautiful flat; I thought you said you'd never leave it. John, what's got into you? Sometimes I think I don't know you at all. How would you possibly manage in a great pile of a house?'

'Well, that's it really – I thought – I thought that you and I – that you could –' He was on the point of saying 'You could move in with me,' but Fiona interrupted, her eyes bright.

'Marry you?'

And he turned from the road and looked at her, and then turned his eyes back to the road again.

'Yes,' he said after a moment. And then he lied again. 'That's what I was going to say. Will you marry me?'

Which proposition Fiona agreed to with no delay.

Grant thought his bank manager looked pale the next time they spoke. At their last interview he had had the distinct impression that the man did not like him, not at all. Bumptious, he would have called him. But on this occasion he was far more complaisant. Yes, the smaller mortgage that Grant now sought could be arranged. There would be no problems.

If he needed anything else, then Mr Grant should just ask. Mr Grant would excuse him if he did not stand up; he was suffering pain; no, Mr Grant should not be concerned, the doctors assured him it was not serious; but he would be going for exploratory surgery and, if necessary, Mr Grant should not hesitate to contact his assistant, who would be able to help.

John Grant wasted no time. The Marchmont flat was put up for sale and quickly, being in a fashionable part of town, attracted interest. At the same time he scoured the property agents for something that would suit him. Here again he was lucky; the recent death of the previous owner and all of his family in a tragic boating accident in Spain, meant that a certain house in Grange Loan, which Grant had often coveted, was up for sale. The asking price was such that only recently Grant would have paled to his roots at the mere thought of it, but no matter, off he went to see his solicitor and made an offer.

Grant's offer was accepted; but there had, his lawyer told him later, been an offer higher than Grant's, which, under the Scottish system of blind bidding he had had no knowledge of, and should have won. But it had been withdrawn soon after the offers had been opened, when the bidder was carted off to hospital after a sudden heart attack.

The seller's solicitor had been, it seemed, distinctly upset. Being a lawyer, he tried to force the sale on the hapless man anyway, but later developments had rendered that course of action impossible and his widow would have none of it. So Grant got the house.

Funnily enough, Fiona did not find the story as amusing as Grant himself, or his lawyer – indeed she was quite upset; but he told himself that she just didn't have quite the same sense of humour as he. Fiona also said that she thought it was unlucky, a statement that Grant found so absurd that he almost laughed, but then silenced himself when he saw a certain steely glint in his betrothed's eye.

He himself was completely untroubled by the fact that his happy state had been attended by, so far, the death of a senior lecturer who stepped out in front of a bus; his father, who had been very old, it was true; the previous owner of the house at Grange Loan, his wife, their three children, his sister, her husband and their two children, not to mention the *au pair* girl, but then Grant had never known them; the anonymous bidder, and his bank manager. Did I forget to mention him? Ah, yes, he died under the knife, poor man; it turned out he was far more ill than anyone had thought.

Anyway, far from being troubled by any of this, Grant thought of it simply as a fortunate chain of coincidence. He saw it just as he saw his uncanny luck at picking winners at horse-racing or playing the stock-market. He had simply become a very lucky man, and why should he complain? And he would be a fool not to make the most of his good luck – after all, he reasoned, it could run out as abruptly as it had run in.

Let those who were less lucky do the complaining; he had no more control, he told himself, over his own luck, good or ill, than he had over the weather tomorrow, so why he should feel guilty was beyond him.

Grant and his beautiful Fiona – and she was beautiful, make no mistake and seemed to grow more so as time went by – were married later that year, and moved into the property at Grange Loan. In the meantime they had had the place decorated, at some considerable expense, which Grant had paid for by a couple of stock-market deals that genuinely amazed his broker, who had begun to put his own money where Grant put his.

At work, too, Grant was fulfilled; and now it seemed that the Professor's job might not be too far away, even though there were a number of other lecturers more senior than Grant in the way.

One day, several years later, as he returned from the Professor's funeral service, Grant happened to find himself in Causewayside.

As he walked, he reflected on how long it had been since last he had walked there and how much his circumstances had changed since he found that book in a little antiquarian shop just nearby.

Suddenly, Grant became aware that he was being watched. It was a most unnerving feeling and he looked around quickly.

Why, there was a man, just at the corner, staring at him, laughing.

Although it was something, that, a few years before, he would never have done, preferring to avoid confrontation, Grant strode up to the stranger. As he drew close, he realised that this man was known to him.

'What are you laughing at?' he demanded.

'At you,' replied the man.

Well that was a little bold, thought Grant. 'Why, do I amuse you?'

'Oh greatly. Don't you recognise me? For I recognise you.'

Grant scowled at him. The worst was, he knew the man was right. They had met. They did know each other.

The man leaned towards him conspiratorially. 'I sold you that book you're so fond of.' He laughed again. 'And I can see that it has done its work...well, half of it.'

'Half of it? What do you mean?'

'Oh don't bluster with me. Don't you see? All that you have now, I once had. Oh, with minor variations. I had career success, tremendous good fortune, a woman I loved and a beautiful home. And all thanks to that Bible.'

Grant stared at him. 'My, that was generous of you,' he said, dryly. 'Why would you give away such a treasure – and so cheaply?'

'Ah well, you see,' said the stranger. 'It hasn't quite finished with you yet.'

Grant was even more annoyed. 'Would you mind telling me what you mean and stop beating around the bush?'

'What it gives, it will take away. Oh, I was once like you. King of the world. And all thanks to that book. I don't have the talent to achieve all that I did, and nobody has that kind of luck. And I can tell by looking at you, that you have not the talent either. I knew that when you walked into my shop.'

'Which you no longer have, apparently,' replied Gant.

'Oh, my dear chap, I have no interest in that trade. I only bought the shop to sell the Bible; and that is what you shall do, or something like it.'

'Oh I will, will I? How can you be so sure?'

'Are you rotten to your very core?'

'Why no! How dare you suggest such a thing?'

'Your appearance. Tell me, do you use a mirror?'

'Yes, of course'

'And what do you see when you look in its glass? A bright, handsome young professional? Comfortable but well-maintained?'

'Why, yes, but...' stammered Grant.

'Then you should look again. Come, see yourself in this glass, this window by me.'

Grant, despite himself, did as he was bidden and looked at his reflection in the shop window. He gasped.

He knew himself to be trim and dapper and well turned out; what he saw was a grossly obese figure, clothes dishevelled, with a malignant air of evil about his scowling face. His fleshy jowls sagged and his eyes were in dark pits. He was, to put it mildly, hideous. 'My God, what have you done?'

'Oh, not I. That book. You coveted it, did you not? You thought it a fine bargain, knowing that it is worth a hundred times what you paid for it; and you thought that your good luck and my bad, did you not?'

'Well, yes...but that's business.'

'That is greed and corruption. You could hardly wait to pay the three pounds and scuttle off with your prize, before I might realise I had made a mistake.' He shook his head. 'Idiot. But no more an idiot than I was.' He paused.

'It is how they all see you, you know; everyone who knows you. They all despise you, but they are too afraid of you and your violent temper to say anything. The tale of suffering that the book has caused, to give you what it has, is etched on your features for all to see, just as they were etched into mine. It has prevented you from seeing what everyone else can, plain as day: that you are an evil, selfish monster who cares only for his own gain. Everyone, from now on, will know what you are. They will avoid you. Perhaps worse, you will know it too. You shall end up alone, ruined and disgraced, with nothing and with no-one.

'And all, all, because you willingly allowed yourself to be seduced. I don't know what horrible things that cursed book did to promote you, how many it killed, how many lived it ruined. But you do. You saw it happening and never once, not once, did you try to stop it. Rather you encouraged it. You thanked it and petted it and polished its cover till it looked like new. And all the time the hellish, malevolent thing was watching and laughing, biding its time.'

'What can I do?'

'As I did. You must lose everything. You must begin again. Those who loved you will not return and those who trusted you never will again. And, of course, you must sell the Bible. But there is a catch.'

'What?'

'You must sell the book for less than you paid for it and you may not give it away.'

'Suppose I destroy it?'

The man laughed. 'Just try. You won't be able to and every injury you infict on it will be repaid, with interest.'

'I shall sell it online then,' grumbled Grant, but the other laughed again and Grant had the distinct feeling that he was rather enjoying this.

'Do you imagine you are the first to think of that? That I didn't try? You fool. You can't choose the buyer – the book will, just as it chose you. That book has been spreading its evil for hundreds of years. You will have to play out the hand that has been dealt to you.'

He paused and sighed. 'And even then, you will have one final task to perform before it finally releases you. And that, my friend, will mean waiting the long years it will take for your successor to do as you have, and I did, and all the others cursed by that infernal book; to have all your wishes granted, and then all your dreams destroyed.'

'What is that?'

'You think I am here out of the goodness of my heart? You think our meeting was a hazard? No. You were *brought* here so that

I might fulfil my final task – to tell you of the fate that will befall you; just as the previous owner told me.'

He moved back and Grant could see some of the weariness lift from him. 'Thank goodness,' he said. 'At last I am done with it. My God, the air tastes sweet – for the first time in years.'

He turned back to Grant. 'Take my advice. Don't try to fight it. The longer you fight, the worse it will get and the deeper you shall be dragged down. That thing comes from Hell itself and it will have its way. Make your arrangements quickly.

'Oh. One last thing. You will not be able to destroy the book. Nor will you be able to destroy yourself. Suicide will tempt you, but you will never be able to succeed. It is a pointless exercise that will only bring you pain and no release.'

With that, the man drew up the sleeve of his jacket to reveal the crisscrossed lives of deep scars, wounds that would surely have killed any other.

'You see, the book owns you; you do not own it. You are its slave. Today, I am free; some day you will be too, one way or another.'

He sighed. It was clear to Grant that the man's humour was improving by the moment, which he did not consider at all seemly, given what he claimed. It almost appeared to be *schadenfreude*... but then Grant remembered how deeply he had drunk from that poisoned chalice, these last few years.

'In a way, you are lucky, my friend. If my recall is correct, it is just four years since you bought the book. Allow another four to break you down completely and destroy everything you cherish, and you might be able to start your life over. As I hope to do, though the time of my rise and fall was much longer.'

'Why have *I* been so favoured?'

The man looked at him harshly. 'Do not mock the Bible! It will have vengeance if you do, that I can promise. Whatever its design is, only it can know. But this I can tell you: it caused us to meet today. Why, I have been searching for you for years, and never found you.'

'I have not been hiding.'

'I know. You were *hidden from me*. There's a difference. But today you walked right into my little ambush, allowing me, at last, to discharge my last duty.' He paused and looked into Grant's eyes. Was there...sympathy, there?

'That means it has already begun to destroy everything that you hold dear. This I promise you: you will have terrible news before the day is out.' With that, he turned on his heel and walked away, his stride becoming lighter with every step.

Grant walked across the Meadows deep in thought. Surely it was just a hoax. This was the twenty-first century. Old books and supernatural curses had no power now. Did they?

By the time Grant reached the foot of Marchmont Road and hailed a taxi to take him the rest of the way home, he had almost succeeded in convincing himself that he had imagined the whole affair.

'Better watch the whisky,' he noted to himself as he paid the driver.

Closing the door behind him, Grant removed his coat and laid it over a chair in the hall. By the table there, where there was still, incredibly perhaps, a telephone, there was a letter. It was addressed to him, but he knew the hand at once: it was Fiona's.

*'My darling John,*

*It is so hard to write this. I am lost, now. I can't live with you and the monster that you have become; a drunkard and worse a violent one. How many times, now, have I tried to leave? On each one you prevented me, followed me, dragged me back, always promising that the drinking and the violence would stop.*

*It never has and I don't have the strength to fight you any more. What happened to the man I fell in love with? What made you what you have become? How could you treat me as you have?*

*I shall never know, and if you are reading this, then it is too late anyway. I have departed this monstrous prison, this daily life of hell, for what I do not know; but it could not be worse than this.*

*Goodbye.'*


With premonition gripping his entire being, Grant ran up the stairs to the bedroom he and Fiona shared. Could he hear water running? Yes, that was it, a trickle of water.

He burst into the bedroom. There was an en-suite bathroom, all tiled in the finest Carrara marble, that led off it. Hardly daring to, Grant pushed open the door.

Fiona was in the bath, dead. She had run it full of hot water and opened her wrists. Her lifeless eyes stared at him, as though accusing.


And in that moment John Grant knew: he was not living through a hoax.


*This and the next story are concerned with the idea that 'crazy people don't know they are crazy'; that for the person living through the events described, they appear very differently to how they appear to others. They look at the question of what happens when a person loses control of their life; loses their 'rational centre'.*

# Testament of a Hanged Man

Some time ago I was rooting around in one of my favourite junk shops when I came across an old briefcase filled with papers.

I asked the owner about it. He said the whole lot was going for fifteen pounds; he had taken it in a house clearance and would have thrown it out, but on second thought, the briefcase was rather well made so he'd put it out to see if it would sell.

'What about the papers inside?'

'I had a look,' he replied. 'Nothing interesting there. Just personal letters and things; looks like some household accounts too. No famous names, well, not that I'd heard of. No money either.'

'Hmmm,' I mused, in a tone that I hoped conveyed sufficient, but not too much, reluctance. It worked.

'Go on then, you can have it for a tenner,' he offered. 'You're always in here, good customer, you are.'

And with that I put my hand in my pocket.

When I got home I set the briefcase on the table by my desk and made some coffee.

The briefcase itself dated, I estimated, from the middle of the 19th century or round about. It was made of a pale tan leather and had two straps and a lock. This lock had been forced, which in one sense was unfortunate, but at least it meant that I didn't have to do it myself. I opened it and began laying out the contents on the table.

As George – the junkshop owner – had said, it was full of papers. Most were, indeed, household accounts. There were some letters, mostly business, referring to various properties in and around Edinburgh. I guessed that our mystery owner had interests in that direction. This was confirmed by another set of accounts, which itemised the rental income from one property, for the year 1859. This property was at ?? Queen Street, in Edinburgh.

The owner of the briefcase, it appeared, was one David MacBeath, a lawyer, who had lived at the same address in Queen Street around the year 1880.

I had almost done, was on my third coffee and was about to

repack the briefcase when I noticed a pocket inside with a fold-over flap. Instinctively – one does – I opened it to see if there was any-thing in it.

There was; an envelope. And by the time I had finished reading its contents the moon was high, my coffee was cold and the cats were out prowling the dark streets of Auld Reekie.


'To whom it may concern; my salutary tale.

My name is Alexander Downie, though my friends know me as Sandy. Alas, I now await my appointment with my doom and commend my soul to the judgement of my Maker. For I am to be hanged here at Calton Prison in my home town of Edinburgh, tomorrow morning.

How often have I noticed the crowds gathered outside this grim place, awaiting the signal that another poor soul has been sent from this life! Little did I ever imagine that I should one day join their ranks.

It is not that I have been a good man. Most assuredly, I have not. I have been an adulterer and a blackguard. I have been indigent and a cheater at cards and even have been guilty of sharp practice in business. But, so help me God, I am not a murderer even though I was convicted of being so and my pleas of innocence fell on deaf ears.

This is an evil place where a dog should not await his death. I am allowed one hour of exercise, in the yard, at a time when the other prisoners are all closed away. So I see no-one save my captors. The rest of the time I am chained to an iron bar on the wall of this dank and gloomy death cell. I have, by dint of begging, been given a few sheets of paper and pen and ink, in order to write down this, my last testiment. I am innocent, I swear before God! How can such calumny have befallen me?


'I was the proprietor of a milliner's shop at the corner of St Andrews Square. By no dint of business acumen did it come to me, as it was bequeathed to my wife, Elizabeth, by her late uncle. To be honest

I hardly knew the man and liked him less, but he, having no off-spring of his own, had left his entire estate – which was not inconsiderable – to her.

I was, I suppose, timely. I had married Elizabeth for want of a better way to secure my future. She was an unremarkable girl, but she had a bequest, enough to live moderately on. She had borne me two children by the time that the events I shall describe took place. Our relationship was cool and, largely, Platonic; although as classical students will know, Plato's love was strictly between two men. I mean only to suggest that the sexual element had quite ceased to be.

I had been working my way through her bequest and wondering how I should make ends meet once it ran out, and at the same time, how to address my bed-chamber problem. Faith I had even considered taking the Shilling and off to be a soldier...well, an officer, of course, as suits my station.

I was saved from this awful fate by the tragic death of Elizabeth's uncle, which left me a choice: to sell the millinery business or to keep and maintain it. It was a nice goose, that brought in enough to keep me, my wife and family in a manner to which I had long aspired; and it came with a spacious apartment directly above. The decision was easy and I lost no time in moving the Downie family into rather more salubrious, not to mention spacious, accommodation than the tiny quarters we had previously rented in the Old Town.

I quickly discovered that the business had another advantage for a man such as I, not overly burdened with a sense of morality; one might say, having none at all.

It came to my notice that the shop was staffed exclusively by young, very beautiful women, with the exception of one Mrs Macready. She was the milliner and also the manager of the emporium. She was older, but remained a handsome woman. I remarked on the pulchritude of her assistants to her one day and she snorted.

'Your wife's uncle was a damnable man for the ladies, I swear, Mr Downie. I'm surprised one of them didn't do for him.'

I pondered this while she looked piercingly at me.

'I do hope, Mr Downie,' she said, dryly, 'That we shall be seeing fewer of the unfortunate circumstances that have previously forced our girls to leave this employ – and all too often, to find their way to the poor-house.'

I just nodded. So it had been that way with the old man? I chuckled.

However, my tastes were not for the young lasses who worked in the emporium, far from it. Mine were for an altogether more sophisticated and worldly fruit; yet it transpired that here too, I had inherited a veritable Aladdin's Cave.

It quickly became obvious, from subtle glances and discreet turns of lips, that my wife's late uncle had been providing a service other than that of purveyor of fine hats.

One such particular, a handsome woman of delicate, long features and sallow skin, visited the shop on a morning in May. She duly tried on a sequence of hats, as I noted from my position beside the counter; without appearing to observe, of course.

Quite tall, around five foot seven; a fine body and a beautiful neck; I imagined in her mid-thirties. I allowed my mind to drift over the subject of the contents of her frock and what warm, delightful pleasures it hid. I confess it was quite the reverie.

I was startled, when, as she signed her account at the counter, she turned to me. 'You are the new owner?'

'Why, yes, ma'am, I have that pleasure.'

'Mrs Whitelaw, you may address me as that,' she intoned. 'And you are?'

'Mr Downie.'

'Of course. You are a comely young man, Mr Downie.'

I could not help but notice how the shop-girls – twittering lassies from Leith, despite their good looks – exchanged glances t this.

The lady was regarding me with a look that was almost predatory; how could I resist?

This is how it began; the tale of betrayal and treachery that led me here, to my Calvary.

Constance Whitelaw, for such was her name, it turned out, was married to a much older man, who had been a colonel in the Indian Army. His family was moderately wealthy and he had significantly increased his wealth on the plundering of the country where he served. He had retired, after thirty-five years soldiering, to Edinburgh and there taken Constance, then a young girl of eighteen, as wife. She had quickly found out that her only expected duty in her capacity as Colonel Whitelaw's wife was to provide him with a son and heir; which she duly did.

After this, it appeared, the Colonel lost interest in pursuing connubial relations with his wife, instead preferring the favours of a succession of Indian boys whom he imported to join the domestic staff.

Constance Whitelaw was not the kind of woman who, having discovered the pleasure of sex,  would shut herself up in enforced chastity, so she began having affairs – and not with crusty old goats with bleary red eyes and the pot belly of too many regimental dinners. Oh no, my darling Constance had an eye for younger meat.

'Mr Downie,' she told me once, as we lay in the sombre shade of her boudoir, 'There is nothing more liberating for a woman in this age than to be married. An unmarried woman is meant to remain a virgin, but no such constraints apply to a married one. As long as she is discreet, well...'

I was happy to become Constance's lover. I was younger than she and this was appealing to her.

Were we in love? I don't know. I became infatuated with her. Who could not have? She was beautiful, sophisticated and skilled in the Rites of Venus. I think she was fond of me rather than loved me. If she loved anyone, it was her son, whom she doted on. But she had sent him away to preparatory school in Perthshire. When I asked about this – Edinburgh is not short of such institutions – she let me know that this was not a topic to pursue, but that, 'Colonel Whitelaw has certain...tastes in the direction of young boys which make me feel more comfortable if our son is out of the house.'


One afternoon I was at her home, a large two-story apartment in Elm Row. Her servants were all loyal and I doubt if the colonel cared anyway. On her bedside cabinet I spied a small box and, without thinking, opened it. (It was only later that it occurred to me that such an action was not only rude but most out of character.)

Inside was a ring, a man's pinkie ring. 'What's this?' I asked, innocently, turning to look at my lover, who was supine on the bed.

For a moment a flash of anger crossed her face; but then she relaxed.

'Oh, it's a ring. I bought it for you.'

'For me?'

'Yes. A token of our love.'

I cocked my head at her. 'I'm very touched.'

'It would not do for you to run away with any ideas, Mr Downie,' she replied. 'But I am rather fond of you. You lack an... experienced hand, but the debauchery has not yet caught up with you. And I rather like your naivety.'

'My naivety?'

She looked at me hard. 'I am your first mistress, am I not?'

I nodded. 'You are that.'

'I thought...that it might be something to remember me by. I bought that ring in a little shop near the Grassmarket. In Victoria Street. Queer little place, I never noticed it before. And I think I should have...Anyway I saw that and I bought it for you.'

'Why thank you, my dear. It is charming. And a lovely thought.'

When I left, later that afternoon, I slipped the box containing the ring into my pocket. I made my way home on foot; it's scarce ten minutes and it was such a pleasant evening.

As I walked westward along York Place, squinting into the orange light of the setting sun, I pulled the box out of my pocket and examined its contents again. It was a simple gold band set with a black jet, oval, and an opal to either side. A handsome ring. I slipped it onto my little finger and smiled. It was a perfect fit. Pleased with my gift I walked on briskly.

As I did so I noted a sudden chill in the air; but it was still April and nights can be cold in the Florence of the North. I shivered and increased my pace. Nothing a little exercise would not cure.

Two or three days later I left the emporium to take my lunch at the Cafe Royal in West Register Street, then a hub of the fashionable and delightful. I had not but closed the door behind me, when something strange happened. Although the day was mild and the sun was shining, I felt a sudden, gnawing cold that seemed to penetrate right to my bones. At the same time, it seemed that a sudden haar had descended, quite obscuring the sun. Edinburgh is famous for these icy North Sea fogs that roll up from the Forth, but they are rare so early in the year. I was just turning up the collar of my coat when a person...it is the only expression I can think of...appeared before me.

It seemed to be a woman, very short, under five feet in height. She was dressed in rags of a strange brown colour. They seemed hardly like clothes at all and much more like filthy old sheets that had been lying on the ground for months. She wore on her head a shawl, so that I couldn't see her face.

I was repulsed by her and I am not a man given to nerves. Yet I could not, try as I might, draw away as she approached. It was obvious that she desired an interview.

I do not know how long we stood, she only a foot or so from me; and then, suddenly, she was gone. I looked around and she was nowhere to be seen; and in that instant I saw that the haar had lifted and the sun was shining again, its warmth slowly penetrating my flesh, that was now chilled through.

I cursed, for I thought I had stood there an hour or more and must have missed lunch; but just as I scolded myself, I heard the report of the cannon firing on the Castle Esplanade, as it does every day at one o'clock. Yet I had noted, before I left the emporium, that it was barely a few minutes to the hour. Now there was a curious thing.

I was quite unsettled by this and even more, by the memory, or lack of it, that I had of the conversation I had with the woman. I couldn't remember a single word that she said. But in some strange way that I could not explain, I understood her intent. She had recognised me. She saw that I bore the ring – the one Constance had bought for me – and that this pleased her; and more, that she desired that I should never take it off.

I was so shaken that I stopped by a beloved hole in the wall for a dram before taking my lunch.

Although I found the ring strangely attractive and was reluctant to remove it, I had decided that it would cause too many awkward questions, were my lady wife to remark it. So, on returning from the Oyster Bar, before going up to the apartment to take my customary constitutional nap, I entered the back office of the emporium, where I intended to take off the ring and leave it in a locked drawer.

It was an odd thing, but the ring – which had slipped so easily onto my finger that morning – was hard to take off. I had removed it more than once already and it had not been so. I wondered if perhaps I had put on weight – but a glance in the mirror gave the lie to that. And in any case, my clothes all fitted perfectly.

Perhaps I was having a reaction to the oysters; but then, I eat oysters almost every day as does, apparently, half the population of this city. But with the aid of a little soap from the wash-stand, I managed to get the blessed thing off. I locked it in my drawer as planned. Then I made my way up the private staircase to the apartment.

That was not the last time I met the strange woman in the stained rags. More troubling was that the ring seemed to be getting harder and harder to take off, though it slipped on easily enough. In fact I even began locking it in the safe, in order that I should not be tempted to wear it. But every time I left the house, despite both my will and not having a clue as to how this happened, I found that I was wearing it.

Every time I went out I was confronted by the macabre woman who, without appearing to say a word, demanded that I should keep the ring. Without her unwelcome persuasion I intended to keep it, since it was a present from Constance and, despite myself, I was growing deeply fond of her. But the woman returned again and again, as if she were not sure whether I would. It was completely clear that she did not want me to get rid of it.

My final straw came when, one day, she approached the door of the emporium. She made no effort to enter but simply stood outside, staring through the window. It was a horrible sensation and eventually I went out to remonstrate. She said nothing, as ever, and as usual I felt the sudden chill and dimming of the sun that always occurred when I was near to her. She just stood there.

I insist, I am not a ruffian but I do confess: such was my sense of frustration with this bizarre woman that I laid hands on her to push her away. I immediately wished I had not. The sensation was... ghastly. I have never felt anything like it.

Her body, though it had the feel of physical substance, was not firm, and felt more like feather pillows under her clothes, or perhaps some other sort of more repugnant and unknown substance. This sensation was so horrifying that I drew back and, for the very first time, she let drop the shawl that had hitherto covered her face.

I cannot describe the full horror of what I saw. Her face was crisscrossed with cuts, open, but not bleeding. One of her eyes was white and blind, But worst of all, most chilling of all, was that the skin – what was left of it – of her face, did not seem like skin at all... more like some strange material that might cover the face of a doll... but no doll so hideous or malevolent could ever, surely, have been conceived of.

I turned away, my knuckle to my mouth, feeling my entrails revolt, and I bent forward, losing the battle. I vomited into the gutter. When I straightened up again, the woman had gone and a small group had gathered around me, looking at me strangely.

At that I felt soft hands on my shoulders. It was Mrs Macready, the doughty manager of the emporium. I had never been so pleased to see her face.

'Come, come, Mr Downie,' she insisted, gently. 'Let's go back inside, now. You'll be catching your death of cold here, without even a jacket on.'

To the crowd – who had begun to grumble disapprovingly – she soothed, 'Mr Downie has not been himself of late; I am sure it will pass.' And into the interior she shouted 'Kirsty! Kirsty! Fetch a pail of water and clean up this mess, would you? There's a good girl.'


That was the last time I saw the woman...save one. But we shall come to that ill moment in due course. From that point on, I was able to come and go as I pleased, with never a sight of the hideous apparition – for I was convinced, despite my rational bent, that what I had encountered was not of this world.

I knew that I had to speak to Constance about it. I had previously avoided discussing the matter with her, in order not to frighten her. I had, however, remarked that when I visited her, she would glance strangely at the ring and then look away, quickly, as if she did not want me to perceive her interest.

Constance and I had our weekly trysts on a Thursday afternoon. The colonel was invariably out of the house then. He was an aficionado of that quaint game, golf, which had become all the rage. He played at Musselburgh links several times a week, but on Thursdays he and some other ex-military friends took a train to Gullane and played a round there. Of course, this was a much more serious expedition and required considerable refreshment afterward, so the good soldier was rarely back in Elm Row before ten in the evening. This left his wife and me plenty of time to catch up.

That Thursday, I mentioned, as part of our post-coital chit-chat, the strange affair of the woman. I was not prepared for Constance's reaction.

She immediately jumped out of bed and, pulling on her robe, sat at her dressing table, regarding me with a queer, fey look. Then she said something I had not expected.

'Yes. I know. I met her too.'

'What? You know her? Who is she?'

'I have no idea.' Constance moved to the window. She was fretting with her handkerchief and clearly was in some distress.

'You seem exercised.'

''I don't know who – or what – she is, but I did meet her. I should have told you, I know.'

'Really? When?'

'The day after I bought...that ring, I went out into Leith Walk to meet a friend for tea. As I left the front door...well I should say I was accosted.' As she said this, her crystal-blue eyes flicked to the ring, which I was wearing. My hand was above the coverlet and it was in plain sight. Her expression was odd...I should have said one almost of...loathing. I shook myself.

'Accosted? What mysteries you do weave, my dear.' She flashed a smile back at me but I could see that she was serious.

'It was frightening. She was a little, round woman – well I think a woman – dressed all in filthy brown flannel clothes, no more than rags. And her face!'

'What about it?'

'Oh Sandy, I hope most fervently you never have such a fright! She was wearing a shawl, you see, that hid her face. But then she raised it and ...oh!'

'What?'

'My dear, she was surpassingly ugly, with her face all puffed up and criss-crossed with lines like scars...as if someone had slashed her, repeatedly, with a sharp knife. It was the most awful thing to behold. And her skin...it wasn't like skin at all. More like, I don't know...the face of a doll.'

'I'll warrant that would give you a fright, all right,' I said, thoughtfully, remembering the effect it had on me. At least her recollection matched mine; it made it less likely that insanity was descending upon me, although the alternatives appeared no better. 'What did she say?'

Constance looked away. 'You know, there's a strange thing. We spoke for an age... I should have thought nearly an hour...but when we parted I could not remember a word she said. And when I glanced at my watch, it said we could only have been together for a minute, if that!'

I moved to her side and touched her shoulder. She was shaking.

'Constance, are you all right?'

She glanced round quickly and I half-expected a rebuke, but instead she smiled shakily and put her hand on mine.

'No, I'm not. It was a most unnerving thing. And she was hideous! I have never seen anyone so frightful...I can't believe that a human could be so ugly.'

'Maybe she was a witch.' It was a bad joke, I knew.

'Oh please don't say that. I'm not superstitious but...Just don't say that.'

'Oh come on, Constance, you're a rationalist! You're always talking about that man Darwin and his theories.'

'Yes, I know...but there was something not right about her... something of the grave.' She shook herself. 'I'm sorry. It just makes my skin creep to think of her with her hideous face slashed to ribbons and one of her eyes all grey and blind.'

I had never seen my lover in such a state before and I moved to change the subject.

'What did she want?'

'I told you, I can't remember what she said. But I know what she meant to say. She meant to tell me to...to get rid of that blasted ring!'

I had not heard her use a profanity before and I was brought up short. Then I laughed bitterly. 'And you did get rid of it – to me.'

'But you insisted!'

'I did not!'

'*Sandy!*' (I had never known her to address me so firmly.) 'You *did!* You – for some reason I don't know why, opened my jewellery drawer and found it...then you insisted that I give it to you.'

'That's not what happened at all! You said you had bought it for me.'

'Well, I certainly did not. I don't know *why* I bought it...it just sort of attracted me. I don't usually buy things like that – and it's a clumsy, awful looking thing.' She shook her head. 'I was amazed that you wanted it at all and you made such a fuss, till I relented and gave it to you.'

I shook my head. My recollection of the afternoon when she had given me the ring was exactly as I have written. This version I did not recognise at all. But Constance as in full song.

'I was so frightened by her, that awful woman, that I took the ring out, meaning to fling it into the Water of Leith. But when I got there, I found...I found I didn't have it.'

'Well you can't have lost it. You gave it to me.'

'That's just the thing. But I distinctly remember putting it in my bag. And I hid it in my drawer so that you should not see it. And you went to it directly as if it had drawn you to it! Sandy, I think it will bring you no good. Be rid of it, as quickly as you can; for I know now that I could not. It has some evil power, that ring.'

I thought about it. 'Where did you say you bought it?'

'In Victoria Street. About half-way down, on the right.'

It would be gratifying to report that the disappearance of the woman from my doorstep, more or less, had brought about an improvement in my humour. But it would be a deception to suggest that it had.

Instead, I was prey to the most ghastly imaginings, of things that were horrifying in the extreme, but not solidified; that remained, no matter how I tried, vague and indeterminate. The worst of this was in dream. I began to wake, in the middle of the night, a silent scream on my lips, rigid and soaked with sweat. Much worse, I began to wake in places *other* than my bed.

One night my wife Elizabeth found me looking through the kitchen drawers for something. She startled me and I came to, from a waking nightmare, it seemed. She was worried and led me back to bed.

We had never been especially close; the marriage was an arrangement that had suited both of us and we were always amicable. Obviously I could not tell her about the ring, for it would have meant revealing the fact that I did not go to my club to play bridge on Thursdays, but engaged in passionate adultery with a woman some years older than both of us and a prominent figure in Edinburgh society.

The scandal would have been disastrous; I would likely have lost my business.

Far from feeling relief, I was filled with an increasing sense of oppression and foreboding which eventually became so intolerable that I believed I was going mad.

I decided to find out more about the ring, so I visited Victoria Street. Sure enough, half-way down on the right there was indeed a shop that sold antique jewellery and such-like. Losing no time I entered it.

Inside was gloomy and somewhat musty in aroma but not unpleasant. There were bookshelves all around the walls, groaning with volumes. Sundry tables, dresses and cabinets filled the centre of the space and on these were placed many diverse objects: clocks, globes, candelabra, ornaments and so on. At the far corner of the shop I found what I was looking for: the jewellery display,

As I gazed into it a woman approached me.

'May I help you, sir? Are you interested in buying?'

'Yes...well, no, but I shall, if you would but answer a few questions.'

'What about, sir?'

I showed her the ring and she frowned. 'Hmm. I know that ring. How did you come by it, if I may ask?'

'It was given to me by a lady friend,' I replied, truthfully.

'I see. And what is it that you would like to know?'

I wondered if you could tell me anything of the provenance,' I replied. 'Would you like to examine it?'

The woman recoiled a little. 'No, thank you, sir. And I fear I can tell you nothing; my father deals with buying the jewellery. Wait for me and I shall ask him to join us. He has a bad back, you know; he's just resting.'

With that she disappeared behind a curtain nearby and I heard her quietly talking, and a man's voice responding. A few moments later an older man appeared, I should guess over sixty, with a shock of pure white hair.

'Good day, sir,' he opened. 'My daughter says you have something you would like more information about.'

'Yes. This ring.' I held it up.

'May I?' asked the man, gently taking my hand. He passed but a cursory look at the ring, then stepped back.

'My daughter says a lady gave it to you?'

I nodded.

'I rather fancy I remember her,' he remarked. 'Tall, very beautiful.' He did not add, 'And married, but not your wife;' but I knew that this he understood.

'Well, then, the ring has little value. Perhaps three shillings. If I recall I sold it to your...friend...for rather less.' The man leaned heavily on his cane, as if a burden had come upon him.

'I don't usually deal in items like that. It came from a house clearance, you see. I took it in with a good deal of other stuff.'

'Can you tell me about the previous owners?' I asked.

'Usually I could not discuss such matters at all, but in this case I can't think it would do any harm. Those concerned with it are all dead, you see, and have been this many a long year.

'I was called upon to clear an apartment in Queen Street. It was one of those huge places that looks out over the gardens there. In fact, being a ground floor apartment, with a basement, it had a tunnel that led directly to the gardens. Very nice, I must say.

'It had been locked up for over twenty years and the lease had fallen due. The Feu Superiors were keen to recover a large sum in service fees that remained unpaid and I was asked to give a price for contents, which I did.' He looked at me. 'But some of the contents were most undesirable.

'You see, sir, the house contained the bodies of the previous owners. They had been there all along and were quite...mummified.'

'What? I never heard such a thing!'

'Oh my dear sir, the landlord and Feu Superiors were at great pains to keep *that* a secret, I assure you. Can you imagine the effect of such news? The house would never have had another occupant and there is nothing more useless to an Edinburgh landlord than an empty property. Normally, I would not be discussing the matter now, but I feel it my duty.'

He looked down for a long moment and then returned his bleary gaze to me. 'Have you, by any chance, encountered a peculiar woman, dressed all in filthy and stained rags, who hides her face under a shawl?'

I started. 'Why yes,' I stammered. 'That is why I came here, to find out more about her.'

'Well, I think I can tell you, but I fear that you will not like it,' he replied.

'I was charged to clear the furniture and personal items and sell them, which I did. That ring came along with the rest. After some time, the strange woman began coming round. I would see her in the evenings. I thought she was a tramp or a beggar, so I made sure she did not enter; lost too many things that way over the years, sir.

'Then, one day, when I was taking my tea in the back shop, she managed to slip in. I heard a strange noise and came out to see; she had forced the lock in the jewellery cabinet and was examining that ring. She was making a strange chuckling sound.

'I lunged forward and snatched it from her, and as I did so, she seemed to hiss at me. As she did, her shawl fell back and revealed her face –'

'Like a doll's face, all covered in gashes!'

'Not a *doll's* face, sir. No. A *mummy's.*'

I felt the blood turn to ice in my veins and the spittle dry in my mouth. That was it, indeed. The face of a walking mummy.

The antiquarian explained, 'I saw the cadavers as they had been found in the house in Queen Street and I recognised her face immediately. One does not readily forget such a sight, my dear sir.

'I pursued some research in the neighbourhood and finally discovered an old lady who remembered the family. She thought they had moved abroad.

'It turned out that the woman had been a somewhat plain and allegedly, so I was told, simple. However, she was possessed of a considerable fortune; she was an only child and her father a wealthy man. She married for love, they told me, but her husband married her for money. He squandered all of it on women and alcohol and gambling. He would not work, so their circumstances became more and more straitened.

'He was a womaniser and an adulterer,' (here the antiquarian shot me another glance,) 'And he would get drunk and beat her. The result of these beatings was that her already far from beautiful features became ugly and twisted. Possibly she herself had recourse to the bottle. Her mind, already that of a simpleton, became deranged and she tottered on the brink of insanity.

'Given that the house was locked from the inside and the bodies all, save hers, lay in their beds, it was easy to piece together the climax. I believe that finally, when one night her husband came home drunk and beat her again, she stepped over that brink, and in a fit of insanity murdered him and her children with a cut-throat razor as they slept; then, realising the enormity of what she had done, she slashed her face to ribbons. Then she wrapped herself in a bed-sheet and slit her own throat.'

He sighed and then went on. 'I should have taken that ring and thrown it into Dunsapie Loch, up on the shoulder of Arthur's Seat. But somehow...I was unable to. Faith, I even went up there one day with that very intention, only to find, when I arrived, that I had forgotten to pick up the ring...when I returned it was in its usual place. Strange though; I clearly remember putting it in a box and then putting the box in my pocket. But when I got to the loch, it was empty.'

'And then my...my friend...you sold it to her?'

'Oh, she insisted, sir. I could not dissuade her. I told her it was a hideous thing and that I had many finer rings, far more suitable for an elegant lady such as she – or indeed her husband, which I thought might be her intention, if you will excuse me, sir.' He gave me a quaint look; I fancy he did not much approve of adultery.

'It was on display?'

'Why, no, sir. I had put it in the drawer of my desk, over there, along with a few other items not worth displaying. But your friend, having looked in the cabinet, insisted that I show her more. So I opened the drawer and she spotted it at once. She would not leave without it. She insisted that she must have it.' He shrugged. 'And so I sold it to her for a shilling, and felt guilty about taking her money.'

'How so?'

'There is evil in that ring and it will bring misfortune; I am quite sure of it.' He sighed again. 'I must say that I have never again been visited by that...woman...since the day the ring was sold. There is no doubt in my mind that they are related. Have you read the inscription on the back?

'What inscription?'

'Oh, it's plain as day. Look, give me the ring and I shall show you.'

I felt an inordinate reluctance to release the ring to him and felt a bizarre anger form; but I controlled myself and handed it to him. Curiously, it slipped from my finger easily, for once.

The antiquarian produced a glass and instructed me to look.

When I did, I saw the words, 'To my beloved Sandy, from Jane. I will love thee till the end of time.'

'Well, I never. Sandy! I can't remember seeing those words before.'

'The woman's name was Jane Rutherford and his was Alexander Smillie. I believe that she gave him this ring – worthless though it be – as a token of her love. And...'

'And?'

'It was clutched in her hand when we found her body.' He paused and then spoke again. 'Sir? Sir, may I ask your name?'

A darkness seemed suddenly to envelop me and I felt an awful chill, such as I had before. I swallowed. 'Alexander. But my friends call me –'

'*Sandy,*' he interjected. 'In that case, sir, I counsel you most earnestly to be rid of that thing at once.'


Little did he know, I reflected, as I made my way back to the emporium, how hard I had tried. Scarce a day had gone by that I had not made up my mind to throw it away, conceiving ever more extravagant schemes by which it would be destroyed; but in every instance, when put to the test, I failed. I would arrive, as the others bearers of this awful thing had, at the appointed place of destruction, only to find that somehow I had forgotten the ring.

Several times, though it was usually extremely hard to remove, it simply fell off my finger without my remarking that it had and when I returned, confused, there it would be, on the floor, or picked up by one of the shop-girls (who seemed quite immune to any influence it may have had) and placed on my desk. On other occasions I literally got to where I had intended to do the deed and then simply could not remember what I had planned to do, only recalling once I – with the infernal ring – was back at home.

I knew then, why the woman had not come back; she had looked into my soul and understood that I could not be rid of her precious ring.

Worse, I began to feel a liking for it. I felt that I no longer wanted to be rid of it. Why, I could not understand that others would call it ugly – hideous even – when it was clearly such a pretty thing. It became the apple of my eye and despite my initial fear, I found that it never seemed to leave my finger. I wore it all the time.

While I was reconciled in this way, my other affairs were not so fortuitous. I found myself frequenting drinking dens that I should never have entered, a mere three months before. And I became short-tempered. I developed a taste for gambling, which soon began to affect my finances, though I paid but little heed. One by one, I let the serving-girls go until there was only Mrs Macready and Kirsty. That was enough; we had surely been overstaffed before.

Worse, I began to bring the anger at my losses in gambling back to the house. I saw that Elizabeth and the children, far from running to greet me warmly when I entered the apartment, now cowered away from me, though I did not understand why. Once I saw that Elizabeth had bruises on her neck and I enquired how she had come by them...she just looked at me with an expression mixed of disappointment and horror, and fled the room in tears.

My relations with Constance, too, fell to a low ebb. We argued frequently, often about the ring that I would wear so proudly. She hated it and pleaded with me to remove it, to get rid of it or, at least, not to wear it while we were together. But I would always mock her and say that this was too unreasonable, since she had given it to me as a token of our undying love; this response just compounded her anger.

In the end, we had a ferocious row. I completely lost control in my fury at her and when I came to my senses, she was beneath me on the bed and my hands were on her throat. It was clear that I had come to not a moment too soon, for she was obviously on the brink of expiry. I leapt back and began to apologise, but it was to no avail. She grabbed the pull by the bed and a moment later her housemistress entered.

'Escort Mr Downie from the house,' ordered my lover. 'And see that he never again enters.'

There was nothing for it; I gathered my affairs and fled the room, the apartment, Elm Row and her life.

My drinking and gambling, which had been bad before, became extreme. Without Constance in my life, my eyes began to wander, but not towards a sophisticated and beautiful mistress, but to the prostitutes who frequented the nether ends of Leith Walk and Constitution Street. I became a great enthusiast for their services; but soon I noted that they seemed to avoid me and on more than one occasion I found myself rebuked.

'Get away from here!' one girl cried; she was quickly joined by several more. 'Aye, you be on your way, mister. We have no need of your silver. We like gentlemen, not your type.'

Soon after that, a number of incidents were reported in The Scotsman newspaper. It seemed that a madman was frequenting the streets of Leith. Several ladies were beaten and the place was in fear; and on more than one occasion, the life of the woman was saved only by the timely arrival of passers-by.

I took no great heed of this, other than to reflect that I should be more careful in my wanderings in that area, since there was clearly a dangerous character present in it.

The matter did not undergo deeper investigation, however, for others came to the fore that, in the end, forced the issue.

The first was that I was served with Sheriff's Officer's warrant to pay an outstanding debt, to one of my suppliers, of fifty-six pounds, twelve shillings and sixpence.

On visiting my bank – only a few doors away – to ascertain why my cheque in payment had not been honoured, the manager drew me aside. 'Your account, Mr Downie, is almost empty. I doubt if you have a quarter of that available.'

I looked at him, aghast. 'Well, could I perhaps arrange an overdraft?'

'Your available funds take account of the overdraft you arranged with us last month, Mr Downie. And that agreement was made specifically so that you could honour this debt. What happened to the money?' He paused. 'In any case, the bank shall not advance you any more, as long as I am manager. You, sir, are a dissolute.'

I left the bank in a state of shock. I had no recollection of arranging any such overdraft. As far as I knew the business had been doing well, and there was no reason why I should be in such a state. Had Mrs Macready been robbing me?

I confronted her with this on my return. Her reaction was hardly what I had expected. Rather it was that of a woman at the end of her tether. She pulled the cash ledger out of the desk and threw it down in front of me.

'Mr Downie, I have been telling you for months that your business is failing. You have let all the staff go but me and Kirsty, and we have not been paid this last month. There are no customers because there is no stock to sell them, and there is no cash at the bank because you, on every close of business, take all that there is and leave a promissory note in its stead.' She held up the bundle of vouchers for me to examine. 'See? Is that not your signature on each and every one? For shame, Mr Downie, would I allow you to take this money from the accounts without signing for it? Why, you might accuse me of taking it – which you appear close to doing.'

I looked. It was my signature, all right. 'I took the money?'

'Yes, doubtless to spend on drink, gambling and women of the street! Look at yourself, Mr Downie! You have lost everything. All you seem to care about is that precious ring!'

She drew back. 'Don't bother threatening me. Violent, you are. But I am not afraid of you. I'll take my leave of you and this emporium – which I have given my best to – and I shall thank you to make up my wages for collection on Friday, else you shall find yourself in receipt of another summons.'

With that, she threw on her coat and hat and left, the tears streaming down her face.

If ever a man needed a drink it was I, after that. I left the emporium and crossed to one of the nearby bars. As I entered I was aware of hostile looks and I distinctly heard a voice quietly say, 'You're well served, landlord, that the law does not allow the sale of alcohol on credit; for here enters the most notorious debtor in the New Town.'

I confess, I may have drunk too much that night. I think I must have fallen down on the way home, for I came to in Queen Street Gardens, outside a vennel that led to one of the houses overlooking it. I could not recall how I came to be there – I had no key for the garden and it was always locked. But there I was.

I looked around and, in the moonlight – for it was by then fully dark – I could make out the legend above the vennel: 'To ?? Queen Street.' Where had I heard that number before? Ah yes, the antiquarian...he had mentioned it. As I pondered this I became aware of a strange glow emanating from the vennel itself. The entrance was closed by an iron gate, which I took to be locked, but to my surprise was not. I pushed and it swung silently open, as if the hinges were newly oiled.

Not knowing why, I entered. suddenly I became aware of a woman in front of me. Her costume was surprisingly unfashionable and she was not a beautiful girl, though one would not have called her ugly. Plain and unremarkable rather. She pressed towards me and I felt her lips on mine.

'So long have I waited for you, my beloved Sandy,' she whispered. 'I shall love you till the end of time.'

I drew back and she laughed – it was not a pleasant laugh. She suddenly turned on her heel and ran out of the vennel, and I gave pursuit. For someone so small and somewhat plump, she was fast on her feet and every time I came close to laying hands on her she drew ahead, as if teasing me.

'Come on, Sandy my love, it is time for us to be together,' she cried, laughing. I knew what it was that I disliked about her laugh: she was insane.

Suddenly I found myself in my apartment above the emporium. It was quite dark. I could see no sign of the girl. I was in the bathroom and without thinking I took my razor in my hand. I could hear a strange cackling coming from the children's room.

I entered and to my horror I saw her, she whom I had come to dread. Dressed as always in her filthy rags, the ghoulish creature of my nightmare was crouching over the children as they slept. She was laughing, and my rage became black as thunder. I slashed and slashed again at her, but she just laughed and laughed and then sprang past me, into Elizabeth's room and threw herself on the bed.

In fury I roared, 'You shall not defile this place, you thing of the grave!' and again I slashed and slashed and slashed until at the end, she lay still before me, a forcibly cracked smile still on her mummy's face.

She whispered, 'And now, my love, we really shall be together, until the end of time.'

With that she melted into nothing and I found myself leaning over the body of my wife Elizabeth, her throat slashed wide open and her face cut to ribbons.

I fled the house and began running, running, through the darkened streets of the city. I did not stop; I ran and I ran until I tripped and fell amongst some trees in Princes Street Gardens, at the foot of Castle Mount. There I collapsed into unconsciousness.

The next morning I awoke to find a group of policemen surrounding me. I had, at that point, no recollection of the events of the night before. They had Mrs Macready with them. Her face was ashen and she was crying.

'Is that him?' one of them asked; he was wearing a sergeant's stripes.

'Yes,' she whispered. 'That's him.'

'Very well,' replied the sergeant. 'Search him for the weapon.'

I found myself held as hands quickly rifled through my pockets.

'Here it is, Sergeant,' said one of the officers, holding up a cutthroat razor, dark with congealed blood.

'Take him, lads. You're under arrest and I advise you to come quietly, Mr Downie. It'll be the gallows for you, I have no doubt.'

I found myself charged not only with the killings of my wife and two sons but with the assaults on several prostitutes.

At my trial, I had no defence. The tale of my descent was told from all sides. The witnesses that I called to speak for me – Constance and Mrs Macready – stated under oath that my behaviour had become increasingly erratic; that I had become violent; that I was a gambler and an alcoholic; that I had ruined my own reputation and squandered my wife's fortune.

Worse, Constance denied all knowledge of the ring or of giving it to me. She claimed that I had made the whole thing up from beginning to end; that there never was even an affair, indeed. She had merely summoned me to bring a selection of hats for her to choose from. She said that she was happily married to Colonel Whitelaw and that I was either mad or lying. Her housemistress corroborated everything she said.

Women of the night were brought forward who testified that I had been a frequent customer and that I was given to violence; publicans from all over town told of how I had been ejected for causing trouble. Even my bank manager swore that on the day of the killings I had threatened him with violence if he would not lend me more money. The police could find no antiquarian shop in Victoria Street at all, and of horrible dead women in grave-clothes, no-one knew a thing. The house at ?? Queen Street was the home and office of a lawyer and property agent, who had taken the lease a year before and knew nothing of the previous occupants. It was hopeless.

The jury did not take long in their deliberations; the Crown was able to paint me as the blackest of villains, a liar, gambler, a frequenter of whores and the lowest dives in Edinburgh, who had squandered his wife's fortune and good name; and who, in the end, killed her and butchered his own children.

At last the judge put on the black cap and pronounced his verdict. I was guilty as charged and would be hanged by the neck until I was dead, at Calton Prison.


And so, here I am. This is my last night on this Earth and I live in dread of the morrow.

I do not fear death, though I doubt if it will be pleasant. I do, however, fear what – or rather who – will be waiting for me on the other side.

*Calton Prison was a notorious jail bult close to the centre of Edinburgh, just to the south of Calton Hill. The conditions inside it were famously appalling and it was considered the worst prison in Scotland.*

*It was built in 1817 and remained in use until 1926, when it was replaced by Saughton Prison to the west of the city. It was subsequently demolished.*

*Executions at the prison, which was Scotland's largest, were carried out at first in public, in front of the building and later within the courtyard. The bodies of ten executed inmates, originally buried within the walls, are believed to still lie under the car park that covers part of the site.*

# Madness and the Irrational Unknown

When I was a child there was no doubt that madness was the most terrifying affliction I could imagine. The idea that one might not just be unable to control one's own life was bad enough. But to think that one *might* be controlling it, but in ways that my conscious mind would never allow, was enough to give me nightmares. The notion that I might be someone other than the sane person I thought I saw, when I looked into the mirror, was simply horrific. The idea of losing rationality and, with it, my central core of *me*, that hub around which my life revolves, has always been more terrifying than anything else that I can think of.

This sense of horror is not unique to me.

We still, today, see people who clearly are suffering from recognised psychological disorders, being subjected to 'exorcisms' – the result of which can often be death – in parts of the world where modern science has not lit the darkness of religion. There are places where to have Tourette Syndrome could be lethal – not because the condition would kill you, but because your neighbours might.

Here in the West, with our arrogant notions of cultural sophistication, the fear is not of the unconscious mind going on the rampage and overwhelming the rational one, but of an external agent doing so. This is typically a demon or other supernatural force; but there is no doubt that the fear of these two phenomena is the same: that of the rational mind being cast down by the irrational.

Supernatural forces do not have to obey the laws of nature any more than mad people have to be rational. Logic, sophistication and rationality are futile in the face of these phenomena; that is what makes them so frightening.

In science fiction, this irrational, terrifying and relentless force is usually alien. Something non-terrestrial, which refuses to obey the rational norms we humans love to think preserve us. From HG Wells' *War of the Worlds* to the xenomorphic anti-hero of the *Alien* films, the terror is relentless. Not only that; it is beyond human resistance.

'Let's nuke them from space; it's the only way to be sure.' In other words, we fragile humans are powerless against such a monster. If ever it comes upon us, we shall die.

This is the key, I think, to the most intense horror writing. As a boy, when I read HP Lovecraft, my teetb chattered at images of dark tunnels where proto-Shoggoths devoured everything before them. Reading the MR James tale, I shivered as a bundle of animated bed sheets relentlessly pursued the narrator along the beach.

I understood then that the horror lies in complete helplessness before the object of terror and its relentlessness. It will never give up. That is all that we know. We can never defeat the unknown. Life is a matter of keeping it at bay long enough to survive another day.

In fact, the fear we experience is of death itelf and that is why it is so powerful. In the first place, self-preservation is strong in all sentient species. In the second, however, our mortality is always known to us. Indeed it is the only thing in life that we may be quite certain of: that we shall die.

Yet of death itself we know nothing. We have invented huge pyramids of fantastical thought, through religion and philosophy, to try to rationalise something we dont know anything at all about. All through human history, the question 'what is death' has stalked us, yet we have never been able to answer it. Death remains at once absolutely certain, yet unknown. It is remorseless and relentless; we cannot escape it forever. The question 'what will happen' will one day be answered, but until it is, there must always be a sliver of doubt, even in the most rational mind. The writers of supernatural horror exploit that doubt mercilessly.

That lovely writer, the late Bruce Chatwyn, speculated on early humans, living in the same caves as bears. He suggested that this might be the reason for our fear of the dark.

While this specific example may not be true, we probably are shaped by evolution to fear the dark. It is the time when we are most vulnerable to predators and least able to defend ourselves. Our principal sense, vision, is least useful when there is no light. It is unlikely that the human tendency towards 'a good eight hours' of sleep is an accident. When we are asleep in groups around the campfire, we are less likely to be eaten.

Michael Shermer has described our propensity to fear the unknown like this: 'Imagine you're out in the savannah and you hear a rustling in the grass. You jump up into a tree and find out it's just the wind. So you feel like a fool. Then again, just suppose you hear a rustling, conclude it's only the wind and carry on; but it turns out to be a lion. Well, you're lunch.' In which case, your genetic line would come to an end. Natural selection predisposes us to fear the unknown.

In other words, we are hardwired to fear that which we cannot know for certain is safe, or even real. And our subconscious mind is the one provoking that fear. After all, the rational mind is saying 'Stop that, it's just the wind', while the irrational subconscious is screaming 'What if it *is* a lion? Get in the tree!'

The foundation of all good suspense writing – and that includes horror – is that fear. What if the baddy wins? What if the branch gives way? What if the hero is seen? What if it *is* a lion?

It exploits our instinct for self-preservation, which, along with our sex drive, is the one of the most powerful stimuli we know. Indeed the successful denouement of a suspense-ridden situation is very similar, in the neurological responses it provokes, to the relief of sexual climax.

These are real emotions and feelings derived from the real world and we experience them in it. Pushing ourselves to the limits, doing dangerous things, adventurous sports, driving fast motor-cycles, even gambling, all produce the same high, the post-coital release.

Writers exploit this. We bring these real-world fears into your home and let you enjoy them vicariously. You can be terrified white as a sheet, and then put down the book and it's done with. You won't fall off the mountain or crash your motorcycle; the baddy will not shoot you and the plane will not crash.

So what makes the difference between the merely suspenseful and the true horror story?

The answer is in the nature of the threat. The risk of falling off a mountain is real and the consequences known; that is why we use the word 'cliff-hanger' to describe a story that uses these motifs. Horror depends on not just the unknown but the *unknowable.*

Because these threats cannot be rationalised, they exist in our irrational subconscious – which we already know is capable of breaking through and upsetting our cosy, rational, conscious mind at any time. Threats are more terrifying when they are not definable, rather than less.

Being able to name your fear tames it. It may still be real, but you will, instinctively, begin to deal with it. You might, instead of jumping into a tree, plant your assegai and face your fear. You can rationalise it, quantify its risk, develop strategies against it – as humans always have done.

The irrational fear offers no such solace. How can you quantify that which cannot be known? How can you develop a strategy to combat it? Of course you cannot.

I am an atheist and a rationalist. I have noticed, amongst some other atheists, a real revulsion against horror stories, especially those which make use of supernatural motifs. For a long time I wondered why this was. Surely, if you don't believe in the supernatural, then it must lose its power to frighten you.

The problem is that we cannot so easily dismiss our inner terrors, our fear of the rustle in the grass. And I think that many atheists, while stoically rationalist, fear this fear itself, indeed more than any other. The simple fact of not being able to define the fear is terrifying; it eats away at that solid foundation of scepticism, as Pascal's Wager, that most dishonest of proposals – that it might be better to believe in god as an insurance, just in case – does. So persuasive, so logical. Yet so destructive, so compromising of rationality, as well as so completely amoral.

I think these atheists fear that the very foundation of their atheism is threatened, in a similar way, by careless talk of supernatural beings – which their rational minds must tell them cannot possibly exist. Quite literally, they fear that this kind of writing may open the door to the insanity of the irrational subconscious mind; and how can they not protest, when they cling so tightly to their rationality, so that they may defend themselves against that insanity. It is a quaint conundrum.


When I was much younger (I am a child of the 1960s) I experimented with LSD, a powerful psychedelic drug. When I was using it, I always stayed inside a citadel that was my rational consciousness. The thrills and highs, the swirling elemental experiences all around me, I enjoyed from within it; but its gate was never broken.

I know, however, from discussions and reading, that others did not do as I did. They threw their citadels open, carelessly allowing the maelstrom around them to take them where it would. I see the same thing in shamans who use similar psychotropic substances; they open themselves up to another world – the supernatural one.

Did I, in some way, miss out? I don't know. Peter Hammill wrote, of LSD, 'I don't make a vital breakthrough and it walks me like a dog upon a lead.'[1] I could never be led in that way, as Peter was; the citadel of my rationality was never breached.

If I did not open myself to the nameless other, however, I did observe it and, in my own reactions, learned about how humans deal with it; we bolt and bar the doors and shiver inside, clutching whichever talisman would keep us safe (Mine was a beach-pebble with a hole through it that I wore on a thong around my neck.)

Horror is comparable to the LSD experience and reactions are similar. The reader will retreat further into the citadel, clutch the pebble tighter; and the writer will redouble his or her efforts to break down the door and snatch the talisman.

I think for the rationalists and, especially, the atheist ones, the citadel and the pebble are mightily important. They are their shields and bucklers. They are mine too, but I have had the experience of seeing at first hand how vulnerable they are.

I must ask myself, 'Why did I not open the gate, let go the pebble?' The answer of course, is fear. And that is why rationalist

---

1 Hammill, Peter, 1973. (In the ) Black Room. Song lyric from the album *Chameleon in the Shadow of the Night*. (Charisma.)

atheists hate the casual use of the supernatural for artistic effect: they fear it.

That is because no matter how strictly atheist we might be, there is a part of us, our irrational subconscious, that screams 'What if it's a lion? Get in the tree!' This time, however, its sense is 'What if I'm wrong? What if it is real?'

The rational mind refuses but the irrational subconscious insists. And that is why supernatural horror stories, which are, after all, about things that rational atheists 'know' cannot possibly exist, nevertheless scare them witless. Like the Turks at the Siege of Vienna, they undermine the bastions of the citadel.

Religious people do not share the same fear. They may be terrified of the monsters themselves, but they have no fear that they might be real, because they know that they are so. They can name their fear and use the appropriate prophylactic – a prayer, some beads, a cross, a pebble with a hole – to counter it.

Their fear is specific, focussed. It has a name. They can see it, describe it. It is not an existential fear in the way that the rationalist's fear of the chaotic madness of the subconscious is. It does not threaten their very understanding of themselves. It might devour them but it cannot destroy them.

I have Filipino friends who regularly surprise me with the closeness they feel to the supernatural world. This is by no means confined to the religious. For example, one friend told me, in all sincerity, how she and her father had to fight off an attack by a *manananggal* – a winged horror of the night that lands on the roofs of houses were there are pregnant women and sucks out their babies through a long, prehensile, tubular tongue.

My friend described in detail the cries of the beast and how the family had reacted. She absolutely believes in the reality of the incident and the threat, and no persuasion will ever shake her.

There is a large housing project in the city of Taguig, part of Metro Manila, called Tenement. In it lives a large group of supernatural beings called *engkanto*. These are similar to the 'good neighbours' of Scottish folklore, or perhaps Irish 'fairies'. (Anyone who thinks fairies are cute little things with wings has not met any Scottish ones; ours eat people.)

The engkanto regularly kidnap children and spirit them away to the parallel realm in which they live, there to become engkanto themselves. Which is all well and good as folklore, and makes a fine story for the two blockbusting feature films made about them; but the fact remains that most Filipinos implicitly believe that they are *real*.

More recently, another friend, a scientist, after pooh-poohing such ideas as manananggal as folk belief, proceeded to tell me how she and her mother had seen a *kapre* while out walking.

A kapre is a mythical being that appears as a dark-skinned man sitting up in a tree; most just watch and they usually smoke cigars.[2] My friend saw no inconsistency between her rejection of the one and acceptance of the other: 'I saw it with my own eyes,' she said.

Kapre do not exist but my friend is not a fool; she is an intelligent, articulate and educated woman. It shows the power that the irrational mind has, that it could make her believe in the impossible.

I am reminded of the yarn in which a colonial type asks an old Highland woman if she believes in fairies. 'Of course not,' she says. 'But they're still there.'


We are not, in the secular West, so distant from these superstitions. My grandmother was a reader of tea-leaves who professed to have the 'second sight' and my mother was as superstitious as any Filipino. I never saw my father so shaken as the time he found me and some friends playing with a home-made Ouija board.

Just because our rational mind says one thing does not mean our irrational subconscious agrees and here, of course, is the seam that horror writers mine so enthusiastically.

What makes this genre different from broader suspense writing

---

2 There is believed to be a kapre in the grounds of Malacañang Palace, the official residence of the President of the Philippines. It lives in a tree near the gate.

is not just the macabre. Horror adds in the disquiet of the unknown and unknowable and this is like a resonator that amplifies its power to cause fear.

It should come as little surprise then, to rational atheists, that similarly rationally atheist writers like me delight in exploiting our subconscious fear of the unknowable and the impossible.

As writers, our purpose is to cause effect; to reach out and touch our audience. It makes little difference whether we are writing a torrid sex scene, a hilarious farce or a chilling horror: we are in the business of playing with your minds.

So naturally we use the tools that are most effective. The fact that one is scared rigid by a story about faceless ghouls doesn't make one any less atheist, it just makes one human. The monster could be an alien xenomorph, a zombie, a vampire, a shape-shifter...it doesn't matter. All that is required is that you cannot name it, for it is that which you cannot name that you fear the most.

Which is of course, why we came to have gods in the first place – why else would the religious call themselves 'god-fearing'? We placed all that we fear into an unknowable supernatural being and then prostrated ourselves in supplication before it. 'God' is both a saviour and a scapegoat; but both are falsehoods, because fear only resideswithin ourselves.

From zombies to mummies to vampires to xenomorphs to deities and demons, our horrors are all the same: incomprehensible, unreasonable, irrational and relentless. We are powerless against them and that is their attraction. We love to be frightened because we love the thrill of relief that comes at the end of it.

*Picture: Charis Fleming*

# *About Me*

I am a Scottish photographer, multimedia artist and writer, with a long career as a freelance journalist and photographer.

I write books on a variety of topics in both fiction and non-fiction. I remain active as a writer, photographer, printmaker and publisher.

I graduated with Bachelor of Art with Honours from Edinburgh College of Art in 1983, majoring in sculpture and also pursuing life-drawing, printmaking and film-making.

After graduation I worked in film-making before returning to photography. I also pursued Journalism Studies through Napier University in Edinburgh.

Both as a photographer and Picture Editor, I presented the readers of the newspapers and magazines I worked for, as well as my, with the very best of photographic imagery.

After publishing news and feature articles for many years, I began to write more intensely in the 1990s . My first book, *Poaching the River,* was published in 2006. This was written in Angus Scots, and was a homage to my home and upbringing in Scotland.

In 2009 I published my second full-length book, *The Warm Pink Jelly Express Train.*

I fulfilled an ambition I had held for many years and graduated with a Master of Fine Art degree from Dundee University in 2011, where my practical area was photography and printmaking, especially photogravure, and my Dissertation was on Goddess culture.

At the end of 2011 I returned to France and began to focus more on writing.

# Books by Rod Fleming

*French Onion Soup!* ISBN: 978-0-9565007-3-1

*French Onion Soup!* is about about the intrepid Fleming family arriving in France, wine, food, the *affouage*—a unique way of gathering winter fuel—French lawyers, renegade mules and many other areas of Burgundian life, in a quirky and hilariously funny style.

*Croutons and Cheese!* ISBN: 978-0-9572612-4-2

The ongoing adventures of the Fleming family in France. This hilrious book has bulls in the back passage, throat holder-uppers, green poo, flaming Daimlers, flying cats and much more to keep you amused from cover to cover. Pour youself a nice glass of Burgaundy and enjoy!

*Why Men Made God.* ISBN: 978-0-9572612-2-8

The Egyptians, Greeks, Romans, Celts and northern Europeans all had pantheons of gods and goddesses. What changed and led to the idea of just one, all-powerful God? Why was the original Goddess abandoned in favour of a sequence of sky-fathers? Who wrote the Bible and why? What impact does that have on us today?

*Why Men Made God* answers these questions, in a pacy and easy-to-read manner, backed up with science. With Karis Burkowski.

*The Warm Pink Jelly Express Train.* ISBN: 978-0-9572612-3-5

Brian Macmaster is a journalist licking the wounds of a divorce in Paris. He meets a transsexual prostitute who leads him into a spider's-web of intrigue, deception and extortion. *The Warm Pink Jelly Express Train* is a sexy, powerful, relentlessly paced novel that is not only a page-turner but also explores one of the most fascinating taboos of contemporary culture.

*A Kiss for Christmas.* ISBN: 978-0-9565007-7-9

Christmas 1981: Europe is in turmoil, the *Human League* is top of the charts, it's pissing stair-rods in Paris and Johnny MacFarlane has just got back from Damascus with a load of smuggled blood diamonds.

Harry, the most notorious fence in Paris, offers him a special surprise: Hermann Goering's gold-plated 9mm Luger. Johnny goes back to the bar to pay his tab, when he gets another surprise: a bullet. That's when his world explodes.

*The Children of Aldebaran.* ISBN: 978-0-9572612-1-1

The time of the Big People is past and the world is ruled by the Animals. Silas Farsight, a young otter who looks forward to a life as a lawyer in the forest village, is horrified when his cousin is kidnapped by a gang of ferocious cats. With his indentured clerk Stoatwise Cuttleworth, he sets off in pursuit.

His cousin, Magda, is being taken to the Dark City, where an evil beast known as the Great Cat is plotting imperial domination of the Free Animals. Silas must rescue her. His adventures lead him to the Sea Otters, a wild and mysterious people, of whom he knows only myth and legend. Yet it is with them that he will find his own true destiny. A fast-paced and exciting fantasy adventure.

*Poaching the River.* ISBN: 978-0-9554535-0-2

It's a typical sleepy afternoon in Auchpinkie, a tiny fishing village on the east coast of Scotland. But all that's about to change. The action races to its riotous climax, as local hero Big Sandy poaches the River Pinkie in a daring adventure, the public convenience is destroyed by a freak explosion, and the minister is baffled by the sudden religious conversion of two formerly heathenish young lads. *Poaching the River* will make you laugh and cry out loud.

*The Spring Run.* ISBN: 978-0-9572612-5-9

Spring is coming to the village of Auchpinkie on the east coast of Scotland. With it, women's minds turn to romance and men's to something else — poaching. But it turns out these are actually very closely related. *The Spring Run* is a hilarious and charming romantic comedy set in a world full of larger-than life characters. (This is a standard-English translation of *Poaching the River*.)

*Buying*

You can buy my books as paperbacks or as e-books from any good retailer in most of the world, including Amazon, Barnes & Noble, Waterstones and all major e-book retailers.

Alternatively, please navigate to my site at http://rodfleming.com/ where you will find direct links to purchase them online or by digital download.

Visit my Amazon Author page!

https://www.amazon.com/author/rodfleming